The Spiral Arm Stories

Volume One

The Spiral Arm Stories

Volume One

Written & Illustrated by Clifford VanMeter

First Printing: 2017

ISBN 978-0-9983630-2-8

www.patreon.com/CliffordVanMeter

Arctos Media, Inc. 1419 Baker Dr. Kalamazoo, MI 49048

www.cliffordvanmeter.com

Special discounts are available on quantity purchases. For details, contact the publisher at the above listed address.

Introduction

The imagined future of these stories take place 280 years from our own. This puts it just a few years after the formation of the Orion Federation, formed by humans (terrachians) and another spacefaring race called the tir'a. Named after the Orion Spiral Arm of the Milky Way Galaxy where both the terrachian and tir'a spheres of influence exist. Both the tir'a and terrachian forces committed many atrocities and many innocents died in the fierce ground fighting and orbital battles. Both sides also captured and interned civilian populations during that lost decade.

The first two stories act as prequels to my book Vengeance is a Wheel. The last takes place right after those events. I've also thrown in the introduction of Detective Constable Conlin O'Donal of Ceres Station.

I hope you enjoy these new forays into my Spiral Arm Universe.

Whiteout

Bitter cold, cold-blooded killers and 3-meter ice worms make for a deadly cocktail.

The inspiration for this story came from a true tale of one of my personal heroes, President Theodore Roosevelt. It provides just one example of why Roosevelt was a master of badassery —

In early spring of 1886, long before he took the oval office and just as the ice was beginning to break up on the Little Missouri River, three thieves cut Roosevelt's boat from its mooring at his ranch and took it downriver. Roosevelt, out of personal pride and duty as a Billings County Deputy Sheriff, hastily constructed a new boat and chased after them with his two ranch hands. The cold was vicious and the men he was chasing were armed and dangerous.

They captured the culprits just as a storm hit, but after trying to ride things out for a couple of days, and with their supplies low, Roosevelt decided to take the men overland. Sending his companions back to the ranch.

For three days Roosevelt marched the thieves overland in a blizzard. During that time he didn't dare sleep for fear the men would try to jump him and escape. He kept himself awake by reading a book he brought with him, Tolstoy's *Anna Karenina.* Eventually, he brought the bedraggled men into Dickinson, the closest town.

Roosevelt made about $50 bounty for the 300 miles he had covered, plus the three arrests.

From the Chronicles of Messu Sa'dish, Historian to Va'namir VII Emperor of the Tir'a People – A single kind word can warm the long winter months.

It was about five centimeters thick, a piece of the conduit that ran through the bulkhead carrying transit wires from the control console to the engines that drove the small craft through space. The crash had broken it free and sent a spear-like shard penetrating her side, pinning her to the back of the seat of the little insys ship.

The clear plexi-steel canopy of the craft had shattered and the cold was already making the cabin uncomfortable. Federation marshal Danni Jaheel looked down and took stock of the wound. Not much bleeding, the shaft that held her fast had shot through the fleshy part of her abdomen just under the floating ribs and about six or seven centimeters in from the edge of her narrow waist. There was no bowel smell, so she thought it had missed the intestines. She considered herself lucky until she realized that true luck would have had the conduit hit the jump seat seven or eight centimeters to the right.

She looked to her left where her partner of many years was held tight to his own acceleration seat by the shock webbing. His head was turned to face her and she could see that the half-breed marshal was bleeding from a small gash on his high forehead. The thick gray-green ooze trickled down and followed the path of a the deep furrowed scar that ran the length of the right side of his face.

He was unconscious, but his breathing was normal and she could see no other obvious signs of trauma. She tried in vain to reach over and check his pulse, but he was just far enough away to be out of arm's length and the strain of pulling against the restraining shard caused her head to spin and bile to rise in her throat.

After several seconds she laid back into the most comfortable position she could find and called out, "Orion? Orion! Wake up."

She had nicknamed him *Orion* when they were at the academy together, finding the full measure of his name in the tir'a native tongue too difficult to master.

"Orion! Wake up!"

"Hmmm," he answered in a thick, groggy voice.

"Wake up," she said with all the urgency she could muster without tearing open her side again. "Can you move?"

"No," he answered as he leaned back. "Foot pinned."

She looked down and could see where the collapse of the control console had immobilized the big man's left foot and ankle against the deck.

With substantial effort, the marshal worked his other foot up onto the control board in front of him and with all his considerable strength and bulk pushed against the mangled metal. His face became a mask of strain and pain and the bolts that held his seat in place snapped at the pressure. He continued to push with all his might and after what seemed like an eternity, the metal of the bulkhead groaned and gave way to the force.

His foot unpinned, Orion wiggled the ankle to return the circulation and check for injuries. "Nothing's broken," he remarked.

As he stretched his two-meter frame to its full height, he was able to see for the first time Danni's injuries. "Looks like it hurts," he said.

She grinned, "Damn you... don't make me laugh."

"How bad?" he asked.

"Hurts like... like *teri gaand mein hathi ka lund*," she said breaking into her native Hindi.

"Need to get that out," he said, shaking his head. "Can't stay here."

"I can't reach the ship's coms. You?" she asked.

Orion reached across her and flipped the com switches, there was no answering static from the speakers. "Nothing," he said. "Coms dead."

She leaned back and fought to concentrate through the pain. She had pulled up a map of this unforgiving world as Orion had fought for control of their commandeered ship after the storm hit and before the solar winds had rendered the computers useless. Danni had a near photographic memory, even without that it wasn't hard to envision the landscape into which they had augured.

"Chasing the crims through that storm wasn't smart," she said out loud.

"Hmmm," replied her partner.

She knew her partner well and understood his meaning. Orion was like a hound with a bone once he was on the scent, he would have followed the fugitives through Hell before giving up the chase. Three crims; Artemis Jabin, his partner Paz Payton, and their komouch bodyguard, had stolen an insys ship from the spaceport after a running gun battle with the two marshals through the streets of Allegan, the capital city of Wren's World, the only colonized world in the Proxima Centauri b system. The big marshal's heavy blaster had injured Payton, but the criminals still managed to get to the spaceport, kill three crewmen and liberate a jump ship.

Arriving at the port just moments behind their prey, Danni and Orion had commandeered a similar sub-light puddle jumper and the chase was on.

Neither ship was armed beyond small short-range lasers used to blast localized navigation hazards, so all the marshals could do was follow. Secure in the knowledge that the crims' ship could not leave the system.

The two ships fought a silent tug of war through Proxima's inner system. The criminals did everything they could to shake their pursuit; bobbing and weaving, zigzagging, trying to outpace the marshals' sensors and lose them in the vast expanse. Orion, though not an experienced pilot, managed to stay with them and keep them just within sensor range. At times gaining on them, meter by meter. After hours of pursuit, they were within minutes of bringing the ship's lasers to bear on the escapees when the ion storm hit.

Both ships were buffeted by the solar hurricane and severely damaged. Their one choice was to make for Proxima Centauri b5, a class M planet at the edge of the system. Habitable in that it had a breathable atmosphere but a mean temperature of minus 20° centigrade.

Even through the dim light, Danni had seen the crims' ship tear a deep furrow in the snow and ice of the winter planet's surface as Orion fought to dead-stick their little ship to a softer landing. In the end, he had failed.

The marshal studied the shaft piercing Danni's side and said, "That has to come out."

She nodded. "Just do it."

Orion pulled a small throwing blade from the collection at the back of his wide belt and cut a piece of the upholstery from his acceleration seat. He rolled the material into a tight tube about five centimeters thick and a third of a meter long, then pushed the finished product towards Danni's face.

"Bite," he said. She clamped her jaws onto the material and closed her eyes.

"On three," he said and wrapped his three fingered hands around the conduit shaft. "One. Two..."

At that moment, he pulled hard and the conduit spear was ejected from her body. Her eyes shot open wide, threatening to pop out of her head. Her jaw clamped down on the rolled material with renewed vigor and she screamed, "Bakrichod!" through her gag.

"You. Said. Three." she gasped, spitting out the now mangled material.

"Hmmm," he replied.

He cut up the side of her tunic taking great care to cause no further injury and revealed the wound. Gently, while ignoring her grunts of protest, he turned her to examine the exit.

"Bleeding," he said. "Not fast, but constant."

"Can you staunch the wound?"

He shook his head and said. "No medikit."

"If there's any juice left in the ship's batteries, you could cauterize it," she suggested.

"Pain." he said.

"Better than bleeding out," she said. "I lived through you pulling the damn thing."

The pain was subsiding now from sharp to a dull throb that shot through her body radiating out from the wound. How much blood had she already lost? Was it the cold from the outside wasteland seeping through the broken plexi, or her exsanguination that had started the tremors she felt running through her body?

Orion worked isolating wires from the ripped bulkhead. When he touched them they sparked like flint and steel.

"Sure?" he asked one final time.

"Do it," she said.

He picked up the discarded material from the deck and re-rolled it the opposite way. She returned it between her teeth once more and he leaned in and held the electrical arc less than a centimeter above the wound. The flesh started to blacken and seal while Danni's muffled screams echoed in the small compartment. By the time Orion rolled her over to deal with the exit wound, she was mercifully unconscious.

Danni's next sensation was the cold on her face. She opened her eyes to find herself encased in the same seat material that Orion had used for her gag. Between her body and the leather-like covering was a layer of something that crackled when she moved. Her arms pinned to her sides by the wrap, she used her chin to lift up the thick seat material and peek underneath. Adhered to the underside of the crude blanket were strips of a chunky semi-rigid material she recognized as insulation from the bulkheads of the spacecraft.

She was just able to raise her head enough to see that she was lying on a makeshift sled; cobbled together from a bent piece of the same bulkhead that had provided the insulation. *He's been a busy boy*, she thought to herself. Orion had positioned the sled leeward of the winds and between her feet she could see drifts of blowing snow already covering the nose of the ruined ship.

A sound from her right caught her attention and she turned to see Orion exiting the spacecraft. Over his marshal's tunic, he wore a poncho of the same material that covered her; a broad square of the leather-like cloth. His arms were wrapped in thick straps of the same material, starting at his palms, so only the tips of his fingers were visible. The bulk of the poncho indicated he'd lined the material with similar strips of insulation to what covered her. He carried an awkward piece of unrecognizable equipment under one arm, and a top tied parcel, like hobo luggage, in his other hand.

"Mind telling me why I look like a human burrito?" she asked.

"Warm?" he answered.

"Toasty," she said.

"Hmmm."

"I assume you have a plan?" she asked.

"Crim ship," he said.

"We shot over them, so they should be straight back behind us. Maybe, ten klicks east," she said.

He placed the bundle and the equipment at the foot of her sled. She could see now that the equipment included a small heating unit and a collection of battery packs rudely strapped together. She shot him an inquisitive look.

"When it gets cold," he said, replying to the unspoken question.

"As opposed to now?"

"After dark," he answered.

Heavy wires had been braided into a thick coil and attached to the head of the sled. He walked behind her and looped the wires around his chest, jerking the sled into motion. She winced at the pain from her wound, and said, "I can walk you know. There's nothing wrong with my legs."

"You walk. The wound comes open. You bleed. You die," he yelled back over the wind as he continued to pull them forward a half-meter at a time through the thigh-deep powder.

She recognized the tone and knew well that arguing would get her nowhere. So she settled into the hard sled, turned her face away from the wind and did her best to conserve her strength.

She must have slept again, the constant stop-start motion of the sled rocking her into slumber. When she did wake, it was because they had stopped for an extended period. Orion was at the foot of the sled pulling power rations and a large thermos from the bundle he'd carried from the ship. They were in a narrow ice cave. Its sloped surface turned straight downward three meters back, but the horizontal shelf they now sat on provided shelter from the wind. Beyond the cave opening, she could see that night had fallen.

Through the crisp cold air alien stars were visible above the horizon and the wind had dropped to almost nothing. *Beautiful*, she thought.

Orion propped her up and loosened her wrappings. "Eat," he said as he handed her a ration bar.

She nibbled the edges of the tasteless chunk of soy and algae, and Orion carefully lifted her tunic and checked the wound. The crude cauterization had held and the bleeding had stopped. Her strength seemed to be returning, and it wasn't the iron rations bringing it back. Orion opened the thermos and held it to her lips.

"I'm not helpless," she snapped at him.

"Hmmm." he said as he put the thermos into her strong small hands.

She gulped the strange tasting water greedily, realizing that she was more thirsty than hungry. She had drained more than half the thermos before she thought to hand it back to Orion so he could partake as well. He pushed it back to her and pointed to the snow pack outside the cave. 'Take what you need," he said. "Water's no problem."

She smiled and quaffed down most of the rest. Orion set aside the thermos bottle and wolfed down his own hard rations.

"How far," she asked as he nestled her back into the sled and wrapped her against the cold once again.

"Six klicks," he answered.

"Ababa!" she exclaimed. "How long were you pulling?"

"Few hours," he answered offhanded.

The idea of Orion pulling a hundred kilos of sled, equipment, and her through almost a meter of frozen powder for hours without pause renewed her appreciation of the big marshal's strength and stamina. Working so close together for so long, it was too simple to forget that Orion was not human. She took stock of him now, easily two meters tall with hard corded muscles, a massive chest, and long arms ending in three-fingered hands with sharp retractable claws. His long hair was worn in a thick braid down his back, but now fell loose around his face, providing some extra protection against the wind. In the dark of the ice cave, she could also see the white nictitating membrane that covered his eyes, a soft glow indicating his night vision was in full play. He'd be able to see in the semi-darkness as well as full daylight in a kind of high dynamic range black and white.

No. Not human, but of everyone she knew, he was perhaps the most human. His gentleness when treating her wounds and the stubborn determination that drove him on through the snow despite all the odds stacked against them. Yes, human in the best meaning. In the best way. He might eschew his human half but for her, Orion would always be human.

He had hollowed out a small bowl-shaped depression in the middle of the ice floor between them, digging down a quarter of a meter or so with his claws. As she watched, he took the jury-rigged heating unit and battery packs off the sled and placed them into the hole. The equipment began to radiate as the packs fed the makeshift contraption enough power to activate its coils. Waves of warmth were reflected up and out from the concave sides of the bowl and back down from the roof of the small cave. Water began to drip from the ceiling and walls, and Orion moved to catch the runoff in the big thermos.

Repeating his words from earlier she said, "Water's no problem."

"Hmmm," he said.

Lifted as she was off the icy floor of the cave, the runoff from the melting walls caused Danni little discomfort, but she could see that Orion was trying to fold part of his poncho underneath to keep his backside dry. Scooting sideways on the sled, she turned onto her good side; the movement caused a sharp pain to shoot up from her wound, but she made room on the narrow contrivance and said, "Hop on."

He moved his massive bulk just onto the raised surface and snuggled close, then pulled his crudely insulated poncho across them both and pointed his back toward the little heater. The hum of the heater and the dripping of the water around them lulled and even Orion dozed fitfully in the semi-warmth.

A few minutes or a few hours later, she didn't know, she felt him move suddenly away to crouch on the cave floor with his blaster drawn.

"What?" she said.

"Shhh." he hushed her.

Orion had sensed some danger approaching, but on the bleak tundra of this icy world, there could be no predators. No life at all. Could there?

From deep within the ice cave, coming up from the pit behind them, a bizarre creature burst forth. It was rough a meter across and white as death; white as the snow all around them. It had no face and no eyes, but a wide circular toothless maw. Instead, hard plates lined the sides of that alien mouth, solid but porous like the baleen of a whale.

Orion took no time to examine the gaping cavity shooting toward him. He fired his blaster, but the creature moved on instinct to the side so the blast glanced off the thick hide just behind the open jaws. Flames rose from the wound as the heat ray dug into the beast's skin, leaving a thick scorch mark, like a huge black finger marring the pure whiteness of it's back.

Orion made ready to fire again, but three meters of the worm now filled three meters of cave and the monstrosity rammed its body into the big marshal. The force threw him across the sled and his partner's body, right through the cave mouth and into the unsheltered cold of the breaking dawn. His weapon lost in the short flight.

Danni fought her wrappings as the worm rose up and seemed to dance in the small cave. Its head scraping the damp roof as it bobbed and weaved like a snake. Under the makeshift blanket, she found her own blaster. A smaller blaster than

Orion's massive military-style weapon, it nonetheless had always done the job for her. Despite the closeness of the gun barrel, she fired through insulation and cloth and struck the worm full in its exposed throat. The heat of the blast, fired too close to her thigh, seared her own flesh. Her wrappings were on fire around the two-centimeter hole her shot had left behind. The monster was also burning, flames spurting from a great gouge in its chest. It screamed, as the fire seemed to consume it from the inside and fell hard across the little heating unit, its weight smashing the crude equipment, bits of electrics exploding out. One hit her face just below her eye drawing a tiny red line in the dusty brown flesh of her cheek.

Orion scrambled back into the cave and used his hands to pat down the tiny blaze still sputtering on her blanket. "Stupid," he said.

"What, I'm supposed to lay here and let it eat me?" she said with sarcasm.

"I..." he started, but she cut him off.

'Or wait for you to come riding to the rescue?" she said. "I'll have you know, I'm no damsel. I'm a marshal same as you. I can take care of myself."

"Hmmm." he replied. Then looking across at the smoldering carcass, "Apparently."

Bracing his back against the cave wall, he used his powerful legs to push the dead worm off the heater and examined the wreckage. Their single source of heat was as dead as the worm and the ice walls and floor of the cave were already beginning to refreeze. Although the sun was peeking above the horizon, it would be several more hours before it provided enough warmth to bring the temperature to a bearable level. Even through the haphazard insulation of their coverings, the marshals could already feel the icy fingers of the air outside the cave penetrating its opening.

Danni pointed to the body of the dead worm, "Look."

Long past the time it should have stopped, the wound of the dead beast continued to smolder.

The smell was not encouraging, but when he placed his hands near the gash Orion could feel some small warmth.

The half-breed drew out the *assu khtra*, the short, single-edged dueling blade carried by all adult members of the tir'a race. Driving the blade deep into the laceration left by the blaster, he pulled down hard slicing through the thick hide of the creature to reveal traces of flame spreading down its gullet. The creature's insides were blubbery and coated in an oily, waxy substance; an alien adipocere that burned slow but returned heat to the small cave.

"Va'annu favors," Orion muttered, invoking the name of both his god and the homeworld of his race.

Orion completed his slitting, pulling the thin entrails from the carcass and throwing them back down the vertical opening at the back of the cave. Spreading wide the three-meter beastie, Orion used one of the surviving battery packs and put spark to the opening. He continued to work his way down the body, setting the worm's full length aflame. The blubber burned slow with a greenish fire and a terrible smell. Orion's more sensitive nose was in particular assaulted, and he drew a wide bandana from one of his pockets and covered his lower face against the odor.

The burning worm did not produce the clean warmth of the heater, but it was enough to take the edge off the rising wind as dim light flooded the now crowded ice cave.

They huddled together once again and bathed in the small warmth their enemy provided.

Once again she slept and only awoke as Orion checked her wounds beneath her tunic and pants. The burn was not serious, little more than an angry red patch on the outside of her thigh. He noticed her eyes open and said, "Could ice it?"

"No thanks," she said with a vigorous shake of her head and a smile.

While she relaced her trousers, he lifted the edge of the tunic to find dried blood around the narrowing wound in her side. It had bled, but just a little, sometime during or after the conflict with the worm. "Too active," he said giving her a stern look.

"Sorry," she replied.

The weak sun was high above the horizon now, lending as much warmth to the day as it ever would. The smoldering corpse that had heated the early morning was now a blackened ruin; hardly more than a thick empty hide.

"Three or four more klicks to the crims' crash site. Assuming we're still headed in the right direction," she said, as he returned their meager provisions to the sled between her feet.

"We are," he said with surety. She had her doubts, but trusted in her partner's confidence and laid back onto the hard metal bed wriggling slow to position her coccyx in its least painful position. She was desperate to relieve herself but held her bladder fast knowing the pain it would bring to move and crouch in the cold of the ice cave. Four klicks at the pace they had been making would mean another three or four hours of trudging through the snow, but she had the hopes of shelter if the crims' ship had been less damaged than theirs. The hard rations of the night before were designed to be fully absorbed into the body and produce no waste. The pain *that* might cause, she didn't want to even consider.

Leaving the relative comfort of the ice cave behind, Orion pulled the sled into the outside air and plunged waist deep into the snow. The heavy end of the sled sank in a few centimeters, but by raw strength, he managed to get them moving. Soon the snow subsided, and he was surprised to find the powder only up to his calves and then barely covering the toes of his boots. They had crossed onto an ice shelf. More treacherous footing caused him to slide on the thick ice just below the snow, but it meant overall easier going. Orion paused after the second time he slid on the hard surface and cut several narrow strips from the bottom of his poncho. Facing the rough insulating material out, he bound the strips to the soles of his boots and stood up on the ice to find his footing much improved. Gathering the cables across his chest once again, he started off at a wolfish trot across the barren surface.

They made better time than she expected, and when they stopped to take water from the thermos two hours later, Danni could see a black speck in the distance that must be the stolen insys ship. She could also see that Orion was sweating from his exertion, even in the cold. He gulped the oddly flavored water greedily.

The sight of the ship, and the chance at their enemy, spurred the predator in the marshal to greater vigor and his wolfish trot now became something just short of a run. Danni believed that he would have gone to a full run, but for the little groans the speed of the traverse elicited from her whenever they hit a bump in the snow. His keener ears had picked that up, even over the sounds of the wind. So, he compromised and set a pace quicker than was comfortable for her, but slower than would produce real pain.

Once they had gotten within a hundred meters of the ship, Orion took shelter behind a high snow drift and peeked over it for signs of life. "No movement," he said to her.

"Go. I'll be all right here for a few minutes," she said. "I shouldn't keep shooting holes in this nice blanket you made for me."

She grinned at him, but he looked sternly back at her, then back to the ship ahead. Quickly he scampered over the soft snow and drew his blaster. Zigzagging, he moved low to make the smallest possible target for anyone on the ship who might have a mind to fire at him.

Within a few meters of the hatch, he threw himself flat on the ground and took stock of the crashed puddle jumper. It was less damaged than the marshals' conscripted flyer, and the nose showed little visible blemish behind the mound of snow piled against its wide flat front. Judging by the state of the exterior it had hit on the back end, nose up unlike their head first crash. The engines were jutting upward at an angle from the surface as if the pilot had used the more reinforced area of the ship to take the brunt of the impact. Sparing the cockpit and its occupants.

"Better pilot," Orion muttered out loud to himself.

Crawling the last meters to the hatch, Orion still encountered no resistance. He stood and flattened himself against the bulkhead, at arm's length from the exterior control panel for the hatch. After a few hesitant seconds, he triggered the hatch to open from his position to one side of the portal. Instantly, the white-hot beam of a blaster shot out of the hatchway searing his eyes. He spun into the opening crouching low and fired without seeing along the trajectory of the original blast.

As his vision cleared he could see the body of Paz Payton seated on the deck near the front of the cabin. The blast had caught him full in the chest and taken off most of his right arm. The wrist and hand that still held the other blaster now lay on the deck several feet away. A look of shock was etched onto the dead man's face, and the pool of blood was already freezing around the new corpse.

All his senses scanned the interior of the ship as Orion approached the dead man. His nose told him before his eyes why Payton had been left behind. The wound Orion had given the man back on Wren's World had festered and become septic. Payton's whole right side, what was left of it, was blistered and gangrenous. Like the marshals' ship, this one had lacked a proper medikit. Orion had killed a dying and delirious man who was barely able to lift, let alone aim, that blaster. The cabin was sheltered, but without power had become cold. The chill must have helped stave off Payton's septic shock and aid in coagulation.

It had let him survive longer than his companions had expected; long enough to take potshots at the marshal. The cold would not offer them the same comfort.

It had been minutes since he'd left, but by the time Orion returned to the sled Danni was shivering with teeth chattering. He lifted her off the hard metal, tucked her beneath his poncho and carried her the last hundred meters, cradling her like a child. Once inside the shelter of the ship, he laid her out on the passenger rear acceleration couch and added his poncho to her coverings. Grabbing the corpse by the collar he threw the body into the snow and sealed the hatch. Remembering the dead man's weapon, he pried loose the cold fingers and seated the blaster into his belt, next to his own, then pulled it out again to check the capacitor clip. Three rounds left, plus one in the chamber. He replaced the smaller weapon and examined his own. He found two rounds remaining. The firefight on Wren's World, then the battle with the ice worm had taken a toll and they hadn't gotten spare clips before pursuing the crims through space. "Foolish haste," he mumbled aloud.

"What?" asked Danni. He hovered over her, adjusting her covers. Her trembling had stopped, but she was still paler than usual. He rubbed her arms to return circulation and some of her normal color returned. "Nothing," he said. "You rest."

"I'm out," she said handing him her weapon. "The worm ate my last round."

"You heard?"

"Nothing wrong with my ears," she said.

"I wouldn't want to face that komouch without a charge," she added. "Nor more like that ice worm." She shivered again at the thought of the bodyguard. The komouch were great bear-like hominids. Though they were provisional members of the Federation, they hadn't quite yet developed FTL capabilities on their own. In hand-to-hand combat against one of their kind, even Orion would be overmatched.

Taking her useless weapon, Orion ejected the empty clip. Payton's blaster used similar capacitive ammo, so he reloaded her weapon with the dead man's rounds. Orion's larger weapon had no way to use the smaller ammunition.

Six rounds between them, Danni thought. Still, if that didn't get the job done the service could have their badges -- to bury with them.

Orion examined the ships' comm, and discovered it had been deliberately sabotaged. "Hmmm." he said.

"They wouldn't want a message to get back that they survived. Even if we hadn't come looking, someone would," Danni remarked.

"Where?" he asked.

"Only one place to go, there's a small Fed outpost south of here; a science station. I remember seeing it on the map," she said. "They'll have iron rats same as us, but for any hope of getting off this ice-hole planet that's the way."

"Arey!" she gasped. "Orion. Those people."

"We can't stay here. We have to get after them now!"

"Hmmm."

At his unresponsive response, she tried to push off acceleration couch and to her feet. Swaying a little, Orion put his arm around her for support as she held to the bulkhead. "It should be about six, maybe seven klicks from here; south and a little west. That must have been where they were making for when they crashed. To steal a fresh ship."

"Already gone," he said shaking his head, an affectation learned from years among the terrachians.

"No, if they're between supply runs they'd have to hold up at the station and wait," she said. "We've got a chance!"

"Hostages?"

"We'll have to cross that bridge when we get there," she grinned at him. "We still have six rounds, plus your blades. I wouldn't bet against us."

"Hmmm." he replied. "No batteries. No heater. No ice worm to burn and night falls."

"Yeah. Okay. You're right," she said with some resignation as he seated her back on the couch. "We'll have to shelter here for the night."

She stood again using the bulkhead for support, and Orion moved to push her back onto the couch.

"Damn it," she said, pushing him away. "I've gott'a pee."

Danni managed to hobble to the comfort compartment all on her own. A feat she was most proud of as she took the throne in the tiny room.

They shared more of the iron rations while Orion cobbled together additional blankets and ponchos by vandalizing the ship's remaining seats and sewing the tough material together with wiring ripped from the control console. He dared not take the bulkhead insulation while they used the ship's hull as shelter from the cold night.

Afterward, they spent the rest of the evening huddled against one another on the couch under the pile of improvised rags. The rising wind rocked the ship while snow and thick ice covered the plexi-steel dome. The interior of the cabin became black as a tomb, but like the interior of an igloo, the frozen covering had surprising insulating properties. Eventually, the temperature rose marginally and they were able to sleep.

The weak sun of the ice planet sent a single shaft of light through the translucent dome of the small ship and specks of dust played in the beam. It was the single indication the marshals had that another day had come to this bleak world. Rising from the couch, he laid Danni's head into the warmth of the seat he had occupied a moment earlier and checked the small parcel they had carried from their own wrecked spacecraft. Now smaller still, a single power ration remained nestled next to the big thermos. He had checked the larder of the insys ship the night before and found that Artemis Jabin and his komouch companion had taken every scrap of food.

Danni's eyes opened and she said, "Last one?"

"Hmmm."

"You take it. I'm not hungry. Not for another one of those reconstituted turds, anyway."

"No," he replied. "You're injured. You need it."

She knew the iron rations had not helped assuage Orion's hunger. The tir'a were carnivores, he needed meat. As a half-human, he couldn't proper digest the nutrients and enzymes of the soy-algae briquets. For a moment -- just a moment -- she considered the frozen corpse outside. It could provide the half-breed with the protein he must by now crave.

No, she thought, shaking her head to drive out even the consideration of it. She knew, even if he could, he wouldn't. He'd prefer to die of hunger before he'd sacrifice his honor.

"Only a terrachian," he said under his breath.

"What?" she said, startled. They'd been partners since the academy, more than eight years in a job where the survival rate was against them, but could he now read her thoughts?

"Payton. Alive when they left," he finished his musings. "Nothing for him."

"They probably didn't expect him to live long," she answered, trying to regain her composure and push the cannibalistic thoughts from her mind.

"Still cruel," he said, drew his blade and cut the iron rat into two unequal parts. He handed the larger hunk to his partner and began gnawing on the smaller piece, "Eat, b'nath."

She smiled at his use of the word for *little sister* in his native language. It was as close as he'd ever come to saying, "Please." She bit into the bland bar without enthusiasm, but without further hesitation.

The extra odd blankets from the ship went to double the thickness of their wrappings, and

Danni walked, with Orion's support back to the sled. She protested returning to the conveyance, but he once again shook his head. "No," he said. "You'll slow us."

As much as she bristled at the thought of riding again, she was forced to agree. Even the shuffling walk from the ship to the sled had left her feeling weak. She'd never make four klicks at any speed. Once again the human burrito, she took her place on the metal bed with Orion as her sled dog.

As they exited the ice field, the snow got deeper and their progress slowed, but Orion slogged on. He had bent some of the ship's conduit and laced it with wires to build rudimentary, if ungainly, snowshoes. With those strapped to his feet, he sank a few centimeters into the snow with each step. Once he fell into a rhythm, he moved at almost the speed with which they had crossed the ice. The wind had died down to a soft breeze, and that also aided their progress.

"Where did you learn all this?" she asked.

"The camp," he answered. Referencing the internment camp where he had spent most of his youth.

"Adapt or die, huh?" she said.

"Hmmm." he replied. Again, Danni understood. He'd say nothing more about life in the camp. Her partner had suffered through most of the war in one of the Humanist relocation and reeducation camps. Little more than prisons for the old, the sick, and the too young to be useful, she knew the reputation for filth and disease those gulags had. She could imagine how hard the other tir'a might have been on the half-breed in their midst. Resourcefulness would have been just one of the survival traits he'd have to master to come out alive after almost a decade.

Orion had been moving at a good clip when they jerked to a halt and he drew his weapon. Twisting around to look ahead, Danni could see a dark shadow against the white landscape. "One of the crims?" she asked.

"Komouch," he answered. "By the size."

Dropping his harness, Orion approached with caution. He needn't have bothered; the komouch was very much dead. Orion rolled the huge corpse and called back to the sled, "Gutted."

Danni realized what must have happened. Jabin, caught without shelter in the cold of the night had killed the big komouch and used his carcass for warmth. It was the ruthless and despicable act of a desperate and deplorable man. "Only a terrachian," she whispered, echoing Orion's sentiments from earlier.

The dim fireball of the sun was already touching the horizon when the outpost came into view. Despite the increasing cold, Orion slogged on. His knees to chest gait would have been comical under less dire circumstances. With darkness falling he didn't even try to creep up on the outpost, hoping against hope that if Jabin were there he'd be too preoccupies with any hostages to be scanning for intruders. Afraid of the bloodbath they might find if Jabin were already gone.

Orion pulled Danni up off the sled and set her on her feet. He encased them in as much of the insulated wraps as he could and they stumbled together toward the mudroom airlock. The marshals drew their near empty weapons, slapping cold-numbed hands to warm them enough to grip properly.

Orion thumbed the hatch controls and the door slide aside. A blast of warm, humid air struck them full in their faces, and Danni sighed with relief. Even if Jabin killed them this minute, her face was finally warm for the first time in days.

Once the hatch had closed behind them, they examined their surroundings. A second hatch at the end of the narrow mudroom was three or four meters in front of them. On the walls of the narrow corridor hung snow gear. Heavy parkas and snow pants, boots and insulated rubberized waders. A cabinet of scientific equipment, most of which Danni could not recognize, stood against the opposite wall.

Holding close to the bulkhead, Orion edged forward and peered through the clear plexi of that other hatch. The corridor beyond was wider but empty. More hallways and doors shot off on either side. "No cover," he said back to Danni. "Plan?"

"Shoot anything that looks like Jabin?" she said with a smile.

"Hmmm."

Using the walls for support, she edged up to join him at the hatch. "Ready?" she asked.

"Hmmm," and they crouched as he activated the door controls.

Keeping low, they hugged the walls and made their way to the end of the corridor. Orion sniffed the warm air and said, "He's this way." Pointing down the hallway to his left.

"Sure?" she asked.

Orion nodded and wrinkled his nose, "He hasn't bathed since he killed the komouch."

Still keeping their backs to the wall, they scooted along crab walking till Orion nodded to a door ahead. Now Danni could smell it too, the undeniable stench of death seeping under the gap at the bottom of the door.

The marshals took positions standing on both sides of the door and gingerly, Orion tried the handle. At the first jiggle, the white-hot beam of a blaster shattered the steel core of the door and scorched the wall opposite.

"Predictable," Orion said.

"Yep," Danni whispered. "He's in there."

"I'll kill these people if you try anything, marshals," came a yell from inside the room.

Danni peeked through the hole the blaster had made and could see some of the room beyond. It was a large room with upturned tables and chairs facing the door. "Sit-rep?" he asked.

"A cafeteria or lounge," she informed her partner. "He's got tables set for cover and the hostages on the floor with their hands on their heads. Maybe a dozen or so."

As Danni watched, Jabin grabbed the arm of the nearest female hostage and pulled her in front, using her as a shield. Holding her by the throat, he put his blaster to her head and yelled again, "I mean it. You two try anything funny and I'll blaze the lot of them."

Carefully, slowly, Orion pushed the door open. It groaned on its hinges and the partners peered around the doorjamb to get a better view of the situation. Danni crouched and Orion stood, holstering his weapon. With the hostage in front and held tight, the big marshal's big gun was useless. The beam was just too wide, and the chance of hitting the hostage was just too great.

The woman's azure tunic and white chevrons indicated she was Federation medical corps and Danni did her best to cover Jabin without putting the doctor in her sights.

"You have him?" Orion whispered.

"No solution," she said. "The doc's squirming too much."

On the floor, she could see another azure and several dark crimson tunics of the Federation Science Corps. She thought, *these people aren't fighters, they're squints. Chances are there are no other weapons on the outpost.*

Jabin was the wolf among the sheep. She shuddered to think of what had been happening here for the last two days with the crim in charge. There were scorch marks and bloodstains on the walls of the room. Sometime before they arrived, Jabin must have decided to prove a point.

Orion held up his right hand and entered the doorframe, filling it almost with his bulk. He hunched forward and cast his eyes down, his long hair falling around his face. He made himself seem as small and unthreatening as was possible for a man of his size. Under his poncho, Danni could see his left hand reaching to the back of his wide belt. He removed one of the small, double-edged throwing knives into his concealed palm.

"That's it, marshal," Jabin snarled. 'Just keep 'em coming. We'll all just sit a spell till the supply ship get's here."

"Hmmm," Orion replied as he shifted the blade in his palm.

"Show me that other hand, marshal, Jabin said. "Or the lady doctor dies."

"Can't. Broken," Orion said. "In the crash."

"Then turn so's I can see," Jabin ordered. "But slowly."

Orion began to turn, rotating his body almost casually and retaining his bowed posture. Just about halfway through the turn he whirled and threw the small blade with devastating force. The short narrow shank entered Jabin's right eye with a wet *thunk* and he spun instinctive away from his hostage, screaming.

Danni fired twice in rapid succession. The first shot taking Jabin in the shoulder and sending his weapon flying from his hand. The second shot caught him full in the chest a split second later. He stood there for a moment, coughed blood, and then fell to the floor staring at the ceiling.

The hostages jumped up and ran for the door, and Danni had to push past them to enter. Orion had already kicked Jabin's weapon out of the dead man's reach; a reaction to his training more than any sense of danger. He crouched down over the corpse and pulled out his knife. Wiping the ichor from the blade on the tattered poncho he still wore.

The doctor kneeled beside him and checked Jabin's pulse. A reaction to her training, more than any hope there might still be life in the man who had held a gun to her head.

The action ended, Danni felt woozy all of a sudden and her gut tightened and gurgled. She leaned against her partner handing him her weapon as he put his arm around her to prop her up.

The doctor added her support and pulled up her tunic to check the wound in Danni's side. Orion could see that it was still blackened, but healing and no longer red. "Her wound?" he asked.

"I don't think so," replied the doctor. "Tell me, did you melt snow for drinking water?"

"Yes," replied the big marshal.

"That's it then. There are microorganisms in the snow pack. It's what the ice worms feed on. For humans it's mildly toxic, like food poisoning. It takes a couple of days to hit. I can give her something to help, but I think the diarrhea is about to set in," she explained.

Danni, still dizzy and now half conscious said, "Well shit."

--- *The End*

WHY THE WEIRWAN?

The marshals are diverted to investigate a most unusual murder.

From the prisms of The Darkness Of The Blue-Gold Sea, poet laureate of the weirwan of the Tidal Pools of Forge: The afflictions, passions, and evils of the intolerant and self-important are rooted in the three poisons; greed, anger, and delusion.

"Why us?" he asked as he squirmed to fit his two-meter frame into the acceleration webbing of the jump seat.

"We're the closest," she replied. "The report that came in claims an, 'existential threat,' to the Federation. I'm not any happier about putting our prisoner into the custody of the ship's crew than you are, Orion, but we go where we're told. When we're told."

"Hmmm."

Her much smaller frame allowed Federation Marshal Danni Jaheel to fold her legs beneath her even in the confines of the webbed seat. In all, she was a compact woman, but muscular and broad shouldered. Standing face-to-face with her partner, the top of her close-cropped black hair would have barely reached the chin of the big man.

Federation Marshal Geos Ah'rion Rassas rel Pen'atha, her partner these last eight years, was a massive individual and would have been uncomfortably constrained in almost any seat he filled. "Don't like it," his deep hoarse voice echoed in the tiny cabin of the massive FTL ship.

"Orion... look," she said modifying the alienness of his name with the nickname she'd first given him at the academy. "I know this one mattered more than most to you," she continued, her striking green eyes softening.

"Grew up in the camps," Orion replied. "Camps like his."

"And you were in one of the better ones, "she said. "Not one where the camp warden was selling off food and medical supplies on the black market. Supplies meant for the detainees"

"Hmmm," he replied.

"Still, he can't jump ship in hyperspace, and the guy's 86 years old now," she said. "He's not going to overwhelm the crew."

"He was ours." her taciturn companion replied. "We're not investigators. We're hunters."

"So we secure the scene and hold it till the investigators get there in three days," she said. "No big."

"Hmmm."

Orion leaned his head back into the webbing and closed his dark almond eyes. They had been transporting their prisoner, Jacob Nangwaya back to Midway, the seat of the Federation Council, to stand trial for war crimes committed while he was warden of a tir'a internment camp on Santo Santiago during the decade-long war between the tir'a and the terrachians.

Toward the end of the war, starvation and deprivations in the camps were rampant, but Nangwaya's camp was one of the worst.

Hundreds of detainees, most old or very young, died on his watch. After chasing him across nine worlds, the marshals had managed to corner the man and take him into custody. Still breathing if not unhurt, though the same could not be said of the two bodyguards who had been supposed to keep the marshals at bay.

Orion looked down and rubbed the scorched line in the palm of his massive, three-fingered hand; the massaging action triggering the involuntary release of his short sharp claws. The bodyguards were little issue, falling quickly to the fast draw of Orion's big blaster. When Nangwaya had attacked the two marshals with a stun rod, Orion had grabbed the lit end of the weapon and taken the jolt through his body before a twist of his wrist had wrenched the weapon away and broken the old man's arm.

Just after they'd turned over the bodies to the local LEO[1]s, and loaded Nangwaya aboard the

---

[1] Law Enforcement Officers.

FTL transport that would take him to stand before a Federation tribunal, they'd received a hyperspace relay that they were being diverted to the scientific outpost on Valtameri to investigate a suspicious death.

Danni turned away to look out the small slit of a port as she felt the bump of the big ship hitting the upper atmosphere of Valtameri. She continued to watch as the ship broke through the clouds and she could see the surface of the planet below. Nothing but blue met her green-eyed gaze; horizon-to-horizon she saw nothing but the great ocean that enveloped this world. Water, a precious commodity across almost all the worlds of the Federation, water as far as the eye could see.

As they continued to descend, the platform of Federation Scientific Outpost 1327 came into view. Like a cork bobbing in a bathtub, the only manmade object to be seen, it rose up as if to greet them standing on stilts almost a mile from the shallow seabed into which it was anchored.

An industrial artificial island on a world with no natural islands or archipelagos of any kind.

Danni watched as a puddle jumper, a small insys transport ship, rose up from the scaffolding of the outpost to meet the massive FTL starship. Like a remora hooking on to a great white shark, it attached itself to the hull of the freighter just ahead of the huge FTL engine compartments that made up the bulk of the starship's mass.

A short few minutes later, Danni and Orion were standing on the upper deck of the outpost, the cool sea breeze on their faces and the sounds of the waves lapping at the pylons below them. Two humans were standing there to meet them. The older man was short and stout. His bespectacled face covered with an unkempt and shaggy beard. The long, stringy fringe of silver hair at the edges of his bald head dancing in the breeze. The younger man was taller and appeared to be of more regular bathing and grooming habits. His dark hair was short cropped and shaved on the sides in a modern style and his face was clean-shaven. Both men wore the dark crimson coverall of the Federation Science Corps, and their shoulder patches reinforced that affiliation.

The younger man stepped forward as the two marshals exited the ramp of the insys ship. "Welcome to Outpost 1327," he said. "I'm Michael Lacey, and this is Professor Hämäläinen, we sent the message that brought you here."

As Lacey was making his introductions, the Professor walked up to Orion and cocked his head at an odd angle. He reached up to his face and raised his glasses to the back of his head, and squinting said, "What are you?"

"Hmmm?" replied the big marshal.

Unaware of the marshal's response, the professor continued his examination. "Far too large for a tir'a, but you have the hands and tusks of that species," he continued. "A human tir'a hybrid, perhaps?"

As he continued his examination, he began to run his hands up and down Orion's left arm. "I've heard of such matings during the war years, but you seem older. Much too old to have come from that period, and you have the markings and the dueling blade of a tir'a warrior. How strange."

"His father was part of the first diplomatic mission to the tir'a homeworld," Danni volunteered. Orion shot her a look as sharp as a tir'a dueling blade and she threw up her hands in a gesture of surrender. "Don't help," he said.

"Ah, that explains it. You must have been among the first. I wonder..." he continued unabashed, "Can you breed?"

At this point, Orion turned his attention back to the professor and gently, but forcibly removed the old man's hands from his arm. Danni, sensing that this would go badly very soon interjected, "Maybe we should turn the focus to why we're here Professor. You mentioned a death and a threat to the Federation?"

The Professor shook his head as if waking from a dream, "Oh yes... yes. My work. They're trying to sabotage my work!"

The Professor turned and went through the hatch and into the interior of the station. "He means for us to follow," said Lacey. "He won't notice we aren't with him till he's nearly to the compartment with the body."

As Orion bowed down to clear the hatchway and stepped over the knee knockers, Lacey turned to him and said," Please forgive the Professor. You're an anomaly, and... well... his mind just doesn't work like other people. He's a bit of a genius in his field, but he doesn't know how to interact with people."

"Just what is your field, Mr. Lacey?" Danni asked.

"His field is linguistics, mine is computer science," replied the young man. "And please, call me Mike."

As they walked down the narrow corridor deeper into the station an aggressive aroma assaulted their senses. Orion's heightened sense of smell was particularly affected, and he coughed and choked as they drew closer to the source. Pulling a large blue and white bandana from his belt pouch, Orion used it to cover his mouth and nose.

"What's that smell?" asked Danni.

"That's the victim," replied Lacey. ""Just through here."

The Professor was there well ahead of them leaning over the scorched body laid out on the deck of the room they were entering. He was pulling back the wet, blue and black stained sheet from the corpse beneath.

"Arey!" exclaimed Danni.

Ignoring his partner's sudden outcry, Orion scanned the room before turning his attention to the corpse itself. The space in which they stood was approximately five meters square. The walls were splattered with the same dried blue ichor that stained the sheet. In one back corner of the room stood the remains of a clear vertical plexi-steel tube, more than a meter wide. The center of the tube had been blown out with some force, and a wide jagged hole gave evidence of the power of that blast. Shards plexi-steel were scattered on the floor and some larger pieces were embedded in the metal bulkheads directly across from the shattered tube.

Orion put his hand on Dani's shoulder, whispered hoarsely through the rag over his face and said, "Always work from the outside in."

"Thought you said we weren't investigators," she replied over her shoulder as he walked past to kneel beside the body.

"Hmmm." he responded.

The Professor was agitated, waving his hands and talking quickly, "You see? You see? An attack on my work; a direct assault on the underpinnings of the Federation itself!"

"Maybe you could take the Professor out for a minute while we review the scene," Danni said turning to Lacey.

"Come on Prof," Lacey said, putting his hands on the Professor's shoulders. "Let's let them do their work."

"Hmm? Oh, yes. Yes."

Lacey guided the Professor out the hatchway and back into the hallway, "We can wait in the lab."

Orion leaned over the body and continued to remove the sheet; a slight sucking sound was produced by the places where the thickened blood had adhered the fabric to the surfaces beneath. He studied the corpse; the victim had been burned but its nature was clear. The wide finned mantle, though badly torn, still covered the pair of large lid-less eyes and the remains of the five, two-meter-long tentacles.

"A weirwan," Orion said looking up at his partner.

"Then these must provide them access to the station," she said as she walked over and examined the remains of the tube. "Transport tubes, filled with sea water when in use." She stuck her head within the tube and looked up and down to see the irises that had snapped shut to hold back the sea when the tube ruptured.

Orion drew out a small knife from among a set of similar blades at the back of his belt. Using the tip he raised up the edge of a bit of torn and blackened fabric that had once wrapped the mantle. The little that was left showed dark crimson. "Federation Science Corps," Orion said to no one in particular.

"Severe burns by the looks of it," Danni said. "The explosion was inside out, otherwise I'd say a blaster. How do you burn up and blow up a species that can't leave the water?"

Standing, Orion said, "Good question. Help me roll him."

Though accustomed to the stench by now, the two marshals were struck anew by the combined bouquet of decaying and burnt weirwan flesh. "Fried calamari," Danni said, covering her mouth and nose with her cupped hand. Orion raised one eyebrow at her insensitivity to the death of a sentient. "What? Too soon?" she asked.

The back of the weirwan scientist was as acutely scorched as the front, but not ripped up as bad.

"Whatever burned him, burned him all over, but this is the side facing away from the blast," Danni said.

Orion did not hear her remarks, despite the smell and the pool of half-dried fluids underneath the corpse; he was bent down examining the floor with the tip of that small knife and bandanna to his face once again. As he pushed aside the bits of flesh using the blade, he separated several broken pieces of clear material much smaller than the transparent plexi-steel shards that lay all around the room.

"What's that," asked Danni.

"Not from the tube," Orion said. "Different texture. More like glass."

Orion stood and walked over to the tube, examining the rubberized o-rings that formed the joints on either side of the iris valves. The upper joint of the lower iris was burnt and distended, while the lower joint of the upper ring showed far less damage.

Orion went back and prodded the glass remains into a small plastic evidence bag, adding a thin twisted length of metal he'd also spotted in the detritus. "Glass syringe, maybe."

"Time to see the squints, then," said Danni. "See if they can tell us anything about what that might have contained." Orion handed the small baggie to Danni, and replaced the sheet over the weirwan while she consulted the undamaged computer screen mounted in the wall just outside the murder room to get the location of the Professor's lab.

As they approached the corridor that led to the lab, Orion pushed one hand against Danni's chest to stop her. With the other hand, he raised a finger to his lips. "Shhh, he hissed; pointing to his ears and then ahead to the lab.

From the lab Orion's superior hearing had picked up the sound of raised voices, muffled by the steel of the bulkhead. The Professor's animated voice and that of another man, indistinct as it was it was, it was not Lacey. This voice was deeper, and expressing extreme unhappiness with recent events.

They drew closer and the marshals began to pick out bits of the conversation taking place inside. "... Before you make any accusations against my techneers," the louder, deeper voice said in an angry tone.

"Mouth breathers!" replied the Professor, his voice almost shrill. "Who else? It had to be human. Something was introduced into the tube, that much is plain. Yes. Yes. Only one of your simians could have done such. You could have set back my research for years."

A sudden crash brought the conversation to an end and prompted the marshals to rush the door, hands on their weapons. Inside the lab, they saw Lacey helping the professor to his feet, an overturned table and equipment scattered on the floor behind them.

Towering over them stood another terrachian, his hands at his sides, but a fierce look of anger still coloring his face. The cyan of the man's uniform indicated he was Federation Corps of Engineers, and the stripes on his sleeve labeled him a chief techneer. He was a big man, Orion's height or a little better. Once well muscled, he had turned soft with middle age. His belly lapped well over his belt and the roundness softening his facial features was enhanced by a bushy beard, once as ginger as his hair now streaked with white.

Danni, by far the smallest individual present at the time, shouted," Stand down, techneer." She moved her hand onto the butt of her weapon.

Shocked at their entrance, the angry Chief's head pivoted toward them and then back to the scene with Lacey and the Professor. He moved away through the hatchway and down the corridor. Orion moved to intercept him, but Danni blocked him saying, "Where's he going to run to?"

"Hmmm," replied her partner. Orion crossed over to Lacey and the Professor and helped Lacey raise the old man to his feet. The whole time the Professor had continued to mutter about mouth breathers and dolts. Lacey brushed the old man off and turned to begin righting the table and taking stock of the damage to the equipment.

"See? See?" the old man screeched. "Look around you. This proves it. Chief Jayne and his men... It had to be. Who else had a motive?"

"A motive for what? Murder?" asked Orion.

"Yes... well no... that is yes, but indirectly" stammered the Professor. "They want to disrupt my work. Destroy what we're trying to do here."

"Why?" asked Danni.

"Jealousy... spite... ignorance... take your pick," said the Professor, composing himself somewhat and adopting a normal tone of voice. "Mouth breathers and luddites have always opposed progress. It breeds fear in their tiny chimpanzee brains."

"A chief techneer isn't going to be a luddite," said Danni. "Technology is kind'a their thing, isn't it?"

"Maybe it would help if we explained the purpose our research here," offered Lacey. "You might understand the Professor's... ah... concerns."

"Why bother? They're of the same ilk as that fat rat bastard Jayne," said the Professor. "

"Why don't you try?" replied Danni sarcasm dripping from every word.

"In its simplest terms," began Lacey. "We're trying to develop a universal translator for communicating with the weirwan."

"Lacey, please... you know I hate that colloquial term," the Professor said. "Use the proper scientific name."

"Sorry, professor," Lacey responded. "We're trying to communicate with the Cephalopoids."

"That's what all this is about," said Danni in surprise, "Some kind of lexicon? I thought we had something like that already."

"To an extent, but not a real-time translator," Lacey said. "Communication right now is imprecise and clunky. You see, they don't communicate by sound, but by color shifting the surface cells of their body. Combined with a kind of gesture-based symbolic language using their tentacles that we don't understand very well. They have the most complex language of any species we've encountered."

"Deciphering their language could be the breakthrough we need to achieve deep communication with them," added the Professor. "They are so much further advanced than us in so many areas... chemistry, terra-forming... And their brains... their brains are twice as large by surface area as human's or tir'a. We have so much to learn from them."

"Since first contact, communications have been limited to basic concepts. Just six words... up, down, stop, go, in and out. With those six words we've been able to cooperate and create structures as complex as this, " the Professor waved his arm in the air to indicate the outpost.

"Surprising," said Orion.

"Not really," said Lacey. "Computers use just two inputs, zero or one, just open and closed circuits. Look at the complex structures we can create from that."

"I'm still confused," said Danni.

"I'm shocked," said the Professor mocking. "Let me guess, you don't see how this relates to the dead weirwan in that empty compartment."

"The Professor believes," began Lacey choosing his words with caution, "That this is all about ALMI."

"Advanced Linguistic Machine Intelligence," the Professor interjected. "It's the heart of the translation matrix we're creating. A thinking, learning machine."

"Sounds like AI," said Orion.

"No," said Lacey. "AIs have been outlawed for more than a hundred years, ever since the Doll

Rebellion on Old Earth. This is something different. Something unique."

"You're making the same mistake the mouth-breathers are," said the Professor. "They're here to build the actual circuits of the interface. Lacey handles the software. I provide the linguistic talent that informs the programing. They see ALMI as some kind of threat. That's why they killed *The Violet of the Green Sea.*"

"The what?" asked Danni.

"The Violet of the Green Sea," answered Lacey. "It's the structure of their names; colors, locations and depths. That was his name; he was their head scientist. He and the Professor had been working together for years. They had a rapport."

"And that's why they killed him," said the Professor. "To get at me, to stop my work on ALMI. What other reason would a human have to kill a Cephalopoid?"

"What makes you so sure it was a human?" asked Danni.

"I'm a genius, but it doesn't take a genius to see that the tube was exploded out. Even you and your partner must have sussed that out by now," said the Professor puffing out his chest. "Whatever caused the explosion was introduced from the outside. That means a human agent."

"Maybe this will have some answers," said Danni, holding up the evidence bag and the glass shards it contained. "Can you analyze these?"

The professor looked the evidence bag over, even going so far as to slide his glasses back on his forehead while doing so. Taking the baggie gingerly by its corner he said, "Child's play," and went off deeper into the big room muttering under his breath as he walked.

"Okay. Let's try to get this in some kind of order shall we," Dani said, turning to Lacey. "Start from the beginning."

"The Professor and I were in the lab. I was programming and he was going over some of ALMI's latest transcripts. We heard a thump, almost like someone striking a kettle drum," Lacey began. "I heard it anyway, the Professor becomes oblivious when he's deep in his work. Unless it literally rocked the station, he'd never have felt it."

"So it didn't, "asked Orion.

"Didn't?" replied Lacey.

"Didn't rock the station?" Orion clarified.

"No. A little vibration and that noise was all. Like I said, it didn't even get the Professor's attention. I had to rouse him to go see what was happening. He was annoyed when I disturbed him."

"When you got to that room, was the hatch open or closed," asked Danni.

"Open. Some of Chief Jayne's men were already there. They must have been closer. They had the hatchway open and one of them was loosing his lunch in the corridor."

"And the Professor?" asked Orion.

"You've seen him... the Professor doesn't run. He arrived a few minutes later."

"What happened next?" asked Danni.

"The weriwan," began Lacey, and then paused to see if anyone would object. When neither of the marshals did, he continued, "*Vi*, that's what I called him... he was half-in, half-out of the transport tube. He was still on fire when we got there. One of the techneers had tried to put him out, but had only succeeded in damaging his hands. I had to treat him in the infirmary afterwards. Once Vi stopped burning we laid him out on the deck. When the Prof get there, he put the sheet over Vi and sealed the compartment."

"And that was two days ago?" said Danni.

"Yes. The body hasn't been touched since. With that smell, I doubt you could pay anybody to go in there."

"Hmmm." said Orion.

Danni pushed against the big man's chest till his back touched the bulkhead. Grabing one of his thick braids, she pulled his face down to hers and whispered in his ear, "After all our time together I've come to recognize your, 'Hmmms,' partner. You know something and you're not telling me."

Orion smiled a tir'a smile; jutting out his lower jaw and jerking his head back twice. "The syringe, large bore needle, burnt under water, and one o-ring melted much worse than the other. Murder weapon was..."

"Potassium and liquid sodium," announced the Professor from across the room. "The glass shows traces of both."

"So, for those of us who skipped chem class, what does that mean?" asked Danni.

"Med bay," Orion announced and exited through the hatchway. "You lead," he said as he pushed Lacey in front of him.

At the medical bay, Orion began searching through the supplies lockers till he found what he sought. A thick glass syringe with a 15-centimeter large bore needle. He held it up for the others to see.

"We'd use those to administer something like adrenaline in case of a heart attack, or severe anaphylaxis," volunteered Lacey. "Inoculators are ineffectual for those treatments."

"Fill it with a mix of sodium," said Orion. "Inject it into the tube through an o-ring. Instant water bomb."

"Hai Rabba," exclaimed Danni. "You got all that from a piece of twisted metal and a few bits of broken glass?"

"Makes sense," said Orion. "Irises snapped shut, trapped the weirwan. The tube contained the pressure so the perp had time to escape and lock the hatch."

"And the weirwan fried alive under water," said Danni.

"So, why?" Danni asked as she put the syringe back into its foam enclosure.

"Why, what?" Orion asked.

"Why the weirwan?" she said. "You've got the how, I'm betting you have some idea of the who. What about the why?"

"Means, motive and opportunity," he said.

"Yeah, and we've got a whole bunch of zilch for motive," she answered.

"And where'd the sodium come from?" she added.

The professor became irritated, "Your superiors didn't bother to brief you before sending you here?" he answered.

"No, we didn't have time to stop by the gift shop and pick up the brochure on this place," Danni snapped back. "Why?"

"Perhaps you should talk to Chief Jayne and have him explain the purpose of this station," the Professor answered. "While I have so enjoyed watching the miracle of the pair of you adding two and two and getting four as the answer, I have work to do."

The Professor stormed out with Lacey following close behind. Lacey turned back to the two marshals and shrugged his shoulders in parting without comment.

After a circuitous trip that required them to go up a deck to go down three, Danni and Orion found Chief Jayne in his office deep in the bowels of the outpost.

"Might be easier to show ya than tell ya" Jayne replied to Danni questions about the source of the sodium. Jayne walked them through another set of corridors and down another level still. "We're almost touching the tops of the waves here, just one level above the moonpool," he said.

Danni and Orion could barely hear him over the sounds of the massive machinery churning all around them. "Pumps," Jayne said and pointed to the multi-story tanks rising above the deck.

"De-mineralization on an industrial scale," Jayne continued. "Federation sponsored with human and weirwan technology working in sync."

Danni could see now the reason for the Professor's snide remarks. The huge tanks rising so high above them were labeled Na, K, Cl, S, Mg, and much smaller tanks bore the stencils Au and Ag.

"So getting hold of some sodium or potassium... not such a big deal," Danni said.

""Not 'round these parts," replied Jayne.

"Doesn't narrow the suspect pool much either," added Orion. "Tanks aren't guarded?"

"No. Why would they be?" replied Jayne. "Even the gold and silver ain't worth nothin' less ya can get it off world."

"Hmmm," said Orion.

"So you and your staff... You don't work for the Professor do you?" Danni asked.

"That what the old fart said?" Jayne asked and Danni nodded her head. "Not surprised, he is the center of his own system that man. No, we don't work for the Professor, though we've been instructed to show him, 'every courtesy,' by the Federation overseer."

Jayne waved his arms out to the side and said, "Technically all this belongs ta the squids. We work for them if we work for anybody."

"Then you must know them well," said Orion.

"Well enough, we work alongside them below the waterline," he answered.

"Who, then?" asked the big marshal.

"Who'd have a reason to kill'em?" asked Jayne, then answered the implied question without waiting for confirmation. "None of my men. He'd never stepped out'a line with any of the humans here. You need a motive; you need to look closer to home. His home."

"We know how he was killed, and a weirwan couldn't have done it." said Danni. "Not that way."

"Only a terrachian," added Orion.

"So that's why ya' was askin' bout the sodium," said Jayne. "That's how they burnt him like that."

"Well, the squids have this thing on that one long tentacle. The suckers there have a barb, almost like a little claw. They use that like a whip when they fight. One time when we was diving deep, I seen one'a the youngin's bump into Vi in the dark. He used that tentacle to whip the skin off that boy. Tore him up bad. Just fer'a bump."

"Maybe cultural?" asked Orion.

"Nah," said Jayne. "He was a bully, you could tell by the way they moved 'round him. How they approached him. The other squids were scared of Vi."

"Yeah, okay. Now I'm hungry and my brain hurts," Danni said as they crossed up a level and back down another narrow corridor. Orion had to bend double to avoid the bulkheads in some places.

"The canteen is this way," said Orion, pointing down a darker side corridor.

The outpost ran three shifts, so the kitchen was always open, though the fare was often limited. Danni choose a plate of fried vegetables without asking or looking too close at what they might have been fried in. Orion stepped up to the dispenser and said, "Meat." He was treated to what looked some kind of ground mixture that might once have been part of something's biology, covered in dark, thick gravy.

"Industrial food," said Danni with a snort.

Orion did not hear her; he was already back at the computerized dispenser. As it activated he said, "Same again."

As he returned to his seat at the little table, and between mouthfuls of meat mixture he said, "Opportunity and means... No motive."

"And lots'a motives with no opportunity or means," said Danni, finishing his thought. "Damn, I hate whodunits."

Dani leaned back in her chair and put her hands behind her head saying, "So let's do what we were ordered to do. Make sure the crime scene is properly preserved and wait for the investigators to get here. We've already gone above and beyond."

"No," said Orion, as he finished his meat and by-products tucker. "We've got this."

"Always one of the great poisons; greed, revenge, jealousy, or delusion," Danni said, rubbing her forehead. "That's the basis of all human evil."

"Weirwan, too. I suspect," said Orion. "We need to question them."

"Really?" said Danni with a deep sigh. "That means we'll need the Professor's help and I don't know if you've noticed, but he's not our biggest fan."

"Then Lacey," Orion said. "Either way, we need to dig deeper on the victim."

They found Lacey in the lab, "The Professor's not here," he said as they entered. "He's down at the moon pool consoling the weirwan."

"Consoling?" asked Orion.

"He's been working with them for a long time. He understands a lot of their language and subtle things like moods," Lacey continued. "Even things that ALMI doesn't understand yet."

"That's perfect," said Danni. "We need to question the weirwan, and he can translate for us."

"I'm sure you've noticed, the Professor can be a little... moody," Lacey said diplomatically and he grabbed a small hand-held device with a pistol grip and a 50 centimeter round, flat lighted projector on top. "We should take this, just in case. It's ALMI's remote interface," said Lacey, waving the curious device at the marshals.

Another trek through the rabbit warren of corridors (up to go down and left to go right), brought them to the lowest level of the installation. The moon pool was a large pressurized room with a roughly five-meter diameter opening in the middle of the deck several meters below the waterline. Seawater rose up to a few centimeters below the lip of the pool.

The Professor was sitting on the pool's edge when they arrived. His shoes and socks were on the deck beside him and his pant's legs were rolled up to the knee. His feet dangled over the lip of the pool and into the salty water below. Rippled shadows danced on the steel bulkheads surrounding him as the lights just below the surface of the water illuminated the room and gave his face a grotesque appearance.

"He looks ridiculous," thought Danni and she suppressed a laugh as they entered the room

Around him in the water were three weirwan. Each wore the dark crimson sash and science corps patch on their mantles. Some of their tentacles and large, lidless eyes were above the water and at least one of the individuals had a tentacle around the Professor's shoulders in a way that seemed almost affectionate.

"Females," Lacey said to the marshals as they spotted the weirwan. "Part of Vi's harem."

"How can you tell?" asked Dani.

"After a while, you get so you can recognize them, by the shape of their mantles. Females are easier to spot. They're smaller and have four tentacles instead of five. The males use that fifth one to grab and hold the females during mating," replied Lacey. "Those three are Scarlet of the Copper Shallows, Azure of the Purple Depths, and Teal of the Indigo Trenches."

"That fifth tentacle, is that the one with the barbs?" asked Danni wincing.

"Yeah. You can just about tell how many times females that have mated by counting the scars on their mantles. Some very aggressive males will end up strangling the female if they grip too hard," he said.

"How do you strangle a water breather?" Orion asked.

"They have to draw water through the mantle to breathe," replied Lacey. "If you close off the mantle long enough, they suffocate."

By this time they had reached where the Professor was dangling in the pool and he had noticed their conversation. "What are these two doing here," he snapped at Lacey as he shrugged off the weirwan's caress and stood.

"We have questions for the cephalopoids," said Orion, putting his bulk between the Professor and the assistant.

"This isn't a good time," said the Professor, not intimidated by Orion's size. "They are upset at the loss of their husband and father. Can't it wait, at least until the real investigator gets here?"

"We need to take statements, and it's already been two days since the killing," said Danni.

"Who knows how much has already been forgotten or misremembered?"

At that, the Professor laughed out loud and even Lacey snickered. As he laughed himself into a coughing fit the Professor said, "You idiots, they've told you nothing!" More coughing and Lacey patted the Professor on the back while the old man struggled to catch his breath.

"Stop that you moron," the Professor barked at his assistant.

He turned his attention back to the marshals and said, "The cephalopoids all have eidetic memories, they can't forget anything... ever. That's why they are so upset."

"I don't understand," said Danni.

"You don't understand? I'm shocked... deeply shocked," he said. "They can't ingest him. They can't reabsorb his memories... his knowledge."

The two marshals shared a confused look and it was Lacey who continued, "They normally... well... they eat their dead. By doing so they gain the memories of their departed. Because of the explosion and burns, it wasn't possible to do that with Vi."

"His knowledge is lost to his race, don't you see?" the Professor was getting animated now, and his coughing was getting worse. "They never die. What they are... cough, cough... who they are... cough, cough... just passes on to others of their kind."

At that point, the coughing took hold and the Professor bent double with the effort. Thick greenish mucous streaked with red splatted onto the deck and his breathing came in desperate gulps and wheezes. "Professor?!" yelled Lacey becoming visibly concerned.
"Professor?" Clutching his chest, the Professor fell to the deck and continued to battle for breath.

"Get a med-kit!" Danni ordered and Lacey ran to the hatchway, his rapid footsteps ringing on the narrow metal stairway.

Danni bent down over the acerbic old man and loosened the tunic from his throat. The Professor was barely conscious now, barely able to draw breath at all. Only a thin, shallow wheezing indicated the old man still lived.

Soon even that had subsided, and by the time Lacey had returned with the med-kit, Danni was closing the Professor's unseeing eyes. She shook her head at Lacey as he entered the moon pool room panting and dropped to his knees exhausted.

"Too late," she said and patted his hand in sympathy.

Lacey stood and crossed to one of the lockers that lined one wall of the circular room. From there he retrieved a blue plastic tarp. Unfolding the tarp he went and covered the Professor's body. Orion laid a massive hand on Lacey's arm. "Wait," the big marshal said as he bent low over the body and inhaled deeply through his wide nostrils.

"You've got something?" Danni asked.

"Surely it was a heart attack. The stress..."
Lacey's voice trailed off as Orion took another
deep breath and bent even closer to the
Professor's corpse.

"Toxin," he said. "Lips already starting to turn
blue."

He lifted the old man's face and rolled it in
his hands side to side, searching the area around
the head and neck. Lacey stiffened, as Orion
turned his attention to the man's bare feet and
ankles. "Here," Orion said, pointing to a tiny hole
near the heel of the Professor's left foot. Less
than a millimeter of a thin bristle of some
organic material could be seen sticking out to the
right of the Professor's the Achilles tendon.
Danni reached to remove the thorny needle with
her nails, but with Orion intercepted her hand.

"Don't," Orion said. He reached across the body
and grabbed the med-kit, pulling tweezers from
one of the many pockets in the soft-sided tote.
Using the instrument, Orion removed the spine,
which proved much longer that it first appeared.

Orion dropped the dart into an evidence bag and stood.

"Why didn't he feel that go in?" asked Danni, marveling at the length of the poisonous needle.

"The Professor was diabetic," replied Lacey. "He had very little feeling in his feet."

Orion was looking past Lacey and Danni at the weirwan. Despite all the activity, they did not seem at all agitated but were still waiting by poolside as if the Professor would return at any minute.

"The suspect pool?" Orion asked Danni in a soft voice.

"You're hilarious," she replied under her breath.

Orion nodded to the hatchway the three of them had entered a moment before. Danni moved to the hatch and secured it while Orion triggered the moon pool's outer iris to close. The three weirwan were trapped between the outer and inner closures in about three meters of seawater. As the iris snapped shut, the cephalopoids became very agitated indeed. All except the one Lacey had called Azure of the Purple Depths. She was slowly separating herself from the others, diving down into the pool so that only the very tops of her large round eyes were visible above the top of the still waters.

Lacey looked up at Danni as the hatchway locks dropped in place with a loud clang. His eyes seemed nearly as wide as the weirwan's. Orion could smell the fear coming off him in waves and sweat started to break out on Lacey's face and hands. Orion and Danni shared a quick glance and they knew. It had all snapped into place with the death of the Professor. Two victims. Two killers.

Lacey, in a panic, picked up the portable translator and flashed the words, "They know," to his accomplice. At that signal, Azure launched herself out of the water like a jet engine, water rushing out the sides of her mantle. Fast as his reflexes were, Orion attempts to draw his weapon were thwarted by her crashing her full weight into his chest, sending them both to the deck. Taken off guard by the scene of a weirwan flying, Danni hesitated in drawing her own weapon and that gave Lacey just enough time to grab her wrists and try to wrestle for the gun.

A well-placed knee settled the match between the two, and as Lacey fell to the floor doubled over in pain, Danni raised her sidearm just in time to see that Azure had managed to get one tentacle to the moon-pool controls and open the outer iris. With her other tentacles, she had enveloped Orion and was dragging him into the water. A blow from the tip of her tentacle that was like the crack of a whip sent Orion's weapon skidding across the deck, as Danni tried to line up a shot, any shot, that didn't risk hitting her partner.

By the time she had decided to take the shot, Lacey had recovered enough to grab her legs and locking his arms, tackled her to the deck. Danni rolled on to her back and managed to get one foot free of his grip. She scored a series of well-placed rapid-fire kicks to Lacey's face, but he continued to hold on to the one leg with adrenaline fueled desperation as she finally brought her blaster around and put the tip of the barrel against the top of his head. "I will blow your fucking head off," she said panting.

Lacey released her and rolled on to his back, his eyes already starting to swell shut from her kicks and gave up whatever little consciousness he had left. Danni stood with her weapon at the ready as Lacey moaned and descended into darkness. She looked to the moon-pool just in time to see Orion's hand slip from the side go under the waves.

"No!," she yelled, and she ran to the lip of the pool. All three of the weirwan were gone now, but she could see Orion struggling just below the surface with bubbles escaping from his nose and mouth as Azure's tentacle tightened around his chest, forcing precious air from his lungs. She had another tentacle tight on his waist, blocking him from the knife at his belt. Looking up, Orion could see Danni's distorted image calling his name. Her hand was reaching for him breaking the surface of the pool. Instead of trying to kick his way back to her, he wrapped his free arm around the weirwan's mantle and squeezed with all his remaining strength.

Within a second or two, the struggling pair were lost to the darkness. Danni watched as the ripples of the pool died away leaving a mirror surface, with nothing more than her own reflection staring back. "Orion?" she called.

Leaping to her feet, Danni dropped her gun belt and tunic to the deck and dove headfirst into the pool. She kicked and kicked, diving deeper and deeper, but as the light faded and her lungs burned and ached with the effort she could see nothing but blackness below her. As she turned to make her way back to the surface, her chest felt as if it would rip open and her arms felt sheathed in lead. She barely made it to the surface and clung to the edge of the pool as she gulped the air she so desperately needed. A quick glance showed that Lacey was still unconscious on the deck, but as she worked up the strength to pull herself out of the pool the rush of a wave smashed her face into the edge, bloodying her nose.

"Bakrichod!" she yelled.

From behind her in the pool, she heard a panting gruff voice say, "Language."

She turned, blood streaming down her upper lip and eyes filling with tears to see Orion pulling a hundred kilos of dead or unconscious weirwan behind him toward the rim of the pool. As she pulled herself up to sit on the edge, he half-pushed, half-threw the weirwan up onto the deck, then pulled himself up to sit next to her. She took in a few more breaths of the sweet, humid air then she punched him in the arm. Hard. He barely noticed.

He shrugged and said," You had trouble with the terrachian?"

"He's stronger that he looks," she answered.

Flipping a thumb at the weirwan, Orion said, "Her too."

It took them several seconds to hear the pounding on the hatch over their own laughter. Helping each other to their feet they opened the hatchway to discover Jayne and three of his men standing there. Jayne was holding a very large wrench and his hand was almost bloody from hitting the hard plate of the portal. "What the seven hells is going on in there?" he bellowed and was struck dumb by the sight of the Professor's body. His eyes darted next to Lacey's unconscious form and swollen face, and finally to the weirwan, half out of the water and very dead. Orion had removed his tunic and was wringing out the surplus moisture as he walked over to pick up his weapon. Danni had recovered her gun belt and was strapping it on as she said, "We caught the murderers."

"They didn't come quiet-like, I take it," replied Jayne. Finally finding his voice.

"Some disagreement," remarked Orion, as he brushed back the wet hair from his face.

"The two of them were in cahoots," said Danni when she saw the confusion still clouding the men's faces. "They traded murders to throw us off. It might have worked, but for timing. We got down here sooner than expected. The Professor's death was supposed to look like an accident, but Azure didn't have time to pull this out of his foot." She held up the evidence bag with the needle-like spine, "If we hadn't found this, we would have written it off as a heart attack."

"Well, the old guy was pretty tightly wound," said Jayne. His men nodded in agreement.

Danni kneeled down and rolled Lacey onto his stomach to applied the handcuffs to his wrists. Something, probably the pain of his face against the deck, brought Lacey around at least enough to groan. Spittle ran from the corners of his mouth, and Danni could see that his jaw was broken as well as his nose. Danni pulled Lacey up to his knees, while Orion checked on Azure of the Purple Depths, but she was very much beyond the need of restraints. Azure's whole body was now drained of color. She was a translucent white lump on the deck side of the aperture. "Probably best," Orion said to no one and everyone, "Don't know how we'd cuff her anyway."

Several weirwan were visible in the moon-pool now. From the speed with which their skins colors were changing and their tentacles were waving out of the water, they seemed very upset by the happenings of the last few minutes.

Lacey was conscious now, but doing more groaning than talking. "Show me how to work this thing," Danni said, shoving the translator module in his face.

"Why sheed I," he answered between clenched teeth.

"Because I'm the one standing between you and something for that pain, dumbass," she answered. She reached out and grabbed his jaw. He squealed in pain and squirmed trying to get away. His swollen eyes were full of tears as he

finally managed to say, "Tum
da tiga... tak en da baak."

She looked at Orion, confusedly and shook her
head. "Thumb the trigger and talk in the back,"
he said, shrugging.

Danni went over to where the weirwan had
gathered, five or six of them now. She was't sure
which eyes belonged to which weirwan. She
triggered the portable translator and saw the
screen in her hand light up. A burst of static
erupted.

"Tyhing to al tak at unce," Lacey said, spitting out
part of a tooth. "Pont at un."

Once again, Danni turned and looked at Orion.
"Trying to talk all at once," he said. "Point it at
just one."

As if they'd heard and understood one of
the weirwans, a male by the size of him,
separated from the rest of the pack and came
toward the pools edge. "Why. Kill. I." the

ALMI said through the audio chip in the hand-held device.

Jayne stepped forward and said, "I and Us are the same for them. I think he's asking why Az is dead."

Dani spoke into the back of the device and once again ALMI translated. This time in colors projected through the LED screen on the front of the apparatus. "We had no choice. She killed the Professor and tried to kill my partner."

The male weirwan turned his saucer-like eyes back to the females. Two of them looked familiar to the marshals and as it turned out, were *Scarlet of the Copper Shallows* and *Teal of the Indigo Trenches*; the same two females that had been on hand to witness *Azure's* attempt to kill Orion.

The male soon returned and asked simply, "Why?"

"Lacey killed *The Violet of the Green Sea* and *Azure* killed the Professor."

"We. Will. Devour/Ingest/Eat. Her. Flesh."
replied the weirwan male. "Then. We. Will.
Know."

"It was ALMI," said Orion stepping forth. Danni
stared at him, covered the microphone with her
hand and said, "ALMI? The A.I."

Lacey shook his head, "Not A.I."

"First of the poisons," Orion said. "Greed. ALMI is
priceless to the Federation, but she'd be worth
billions to a Corp."

Lacey, cast his eyes downward and said,
"My wurk. I meed her."

"He made her," said Orion. Anticipating Danni's
look.

"What about her?" she asked, nodding toward
the weirwan's corpse.

"Knowing of Vi," Orion said. "We can guess."

Orion nodded toward the weirwan in the water,
"They'll be certain."

Danni pulled Lacey to his feet by his elbow and the two marshals watched together as the male weirwan's tentacles wrapped around the pale decaying slug that had been *Azure of the Purple Depths* and slid it slowly into the water of the moon-pool.

"Isn't that evidence?" Danni asked.

Orlon shrugged and grabbed Lacey's other elbow. Danni said to Jayne, "Where can we lock him up till the *real* investigators get here?"

-- The End

A Dark & Stormy Night

The night shift in the homicide squad can be murder.

This next story takes place on Ceres Station, the main out-bound port-of-call for the Terran system. Everything coming in from or going out to any of the Federation fringe worlds shifts through huge FTL freighters and smaller insys ships at the port. Ceres Station is the waterfront of the Terran system. Most of it is a dark, seedy, run down, damp and dreary environment — a thoroughly unpleasant place. Permanent residents of the Plutoid world Ceres are known as *belters*.

Our story follows one particular belter; Detective Constable Conlin O'Donal. A broken individual, trying to find his way back to the man he once was.

I pulled up my hood and stepped into the cold and damp. There are always crowds in the streets and alleyways of the Station this time of night. Shift-workers from the manufacturing operations were the making their way home, elbowing past the two and a half meter frames of Komouch dock-wallopers heading down-station for a pint. Everyone is careful of their footing on the rain-slick slide-walks.

Most people wouldn't think of the rain or the rising damp when they thought of Ceres Station. Cold yes. You'd expect that with another 160 or so million miles beyond homeworld, but the wetness; the damn, seeping, dripping, soul-devouring wetness. Nobody expects weather when they're inside, but here it is. "Not rain," I remind myself. Condensation dripped down from the skylights and support struts that touched the outer cold of Ceres' perpetual dusk.

I pause for a moment and look up through those struts and out into the sky. Thin, vaporous clouds drifts by against the inky black of raw space beyond. More like contrails; rising water vapor drifting off the icy surface. The nearest thing to atmosphere our little rock can muster. The brightness of the station lights masks all but the strongest pin-pricks of starscape. A few are still clear, though. Different planes mean different perspectives, so the constellations you'd recognize from Homeworld's surface are hinted at here. Our bright partner glares down on us, the second largest of the sky's lights peeking through our skylights. Nearing perijove now, Jupiter is almost as bright as the sun.

Not so different from a winter's night back home. If your winters happen to be 100° below zero, that is. In the relative warmth of the Station it's easy to forget that I'm standing on a sheath of ice 20-miles thick, over a liquid water ocean, engulfing a chunk of rock surrounded by a million other chunks of rock whirling around the sun two-and-a-half times further out than any human being has the right to be.

One helluva place for people to live.

One of the half-dozen or so gigantic FTL freighters on station at the moment crosses over the skylight and blocks my introspection for a moment, the tiny insys ships darting around it like fireflies. As the ugly underbelly of interstellar commerce slides slowly past, I remember that I have someplace to be. If I want to keep my rent paid and food in my belly, that is.

I step on the entrance belt of the slidewalk and make my way up to the high-speed belt. Within a few minutes, I can make out the squat, rusted and pitted shell of the Van Allen precinct HQ ahead in the perpetual haze. Without being conscious of it, I make my way down belt to the exit lane then slip off the track to step through the entrance and past a handful of uniformed coppers milling about at the front.

Upstairs I step into the squad room, passing hundreds of bits of data lighting up holo-screens scattered around the room like Christmas lights on the holiday eve. Making sense of those hundreds of divergent data streams, that's my job. My gift. Data is not the same as information. Information is valuable; it leads to conclusions. It leads to results. Data has to be sifted and massaged, molded into information. Shaped into conclusions by a *data analyst*, someone who could make sense of all the little bits. Someone like me.

I settle into my cubicle and light up my own vid-screens. "Detective Constable Conlin O'Donal," I say to the ghost in the machine. I envision ones and zeroes zipping through fiber optics, triggering sensors that would check and crosscheck my voice print, retinal patterns, galvanic skin response and God knows what else to verify that I am me.

"Login accepted, Connie my love." came the ghost's reply. A silky, sexy little voice,. A voice so husky it should have been pulling a dog sled. My own bit of techno-sleight of hand; the harsh metallic voice my girl once had, cleverly replaced at my station only.

As I watched the holo-screens sing to life and encircle me, I catch sight of a uniformed constable entering the squad room with a shackled komouch prisoner in tow. The komouch are not especially smart, but their size and massive strength make them perfect for dock or construction workers. We have a good-sized contingent of them here on the Station, but they keep to themselves and stay out of trouble. The human Constable, a man of not insignificant size himself, managed to look like a child standing next to the massive komouch dock-walloper.

The koumuch, the kirkatta, the weirwan, even a few of the warlike tir'a (since the end of hostilities); they all come through here at one time or another. The Station is a gateway to the whole Terran system and from the system out to all the allied worlds. I've been here almost a decade now. I guess that qualifies me as a dyed-in-the-wool, *belter.*

Just as I'm thinking how much I like third-watch, how quiet it is and how nice it is to be left alone, I hear a voice that feels like a cheese grater drawn across my ear drums, "Hey, O'Donal?"

Not tonight.

Detective Sergeant Aackster is the worst kind of copper. Lazy and self-aggrandizing, his focus is on himself. Not solving cases, but *making his metrics.* Clearing cases takes priority over finding the truth. Even over finding the guilty. The shame of the system is that he's gotten away with it all these years and been rewarded with promotions along the way.

His partner, DC Brasher seemed like a good kid. Fresh-faced and eager, I hoped for his sake that Aackster's cynicism and shallowness wouldn't rub off.

"I was just tellin' Brasher here, how you used to be such a big shot back in the day," he snarled as he and Brasher crossed over from the coffee machine. "I just don't think he quite believed me."

I averted my eyes, staring at the steam rising from his coffee cup instead of raising my gaze to meet his. "Is there something I can do for you DS Aackster?" The question carried no intonation, no invitation to answer. A more subtle man would have realized it as rhetorical; an open invitation to piss off.

Aackster, on the other hand, had all the subtly of an enema, "I don't know, O'Donal. Remind me what it is you do around here again?"

"I'm a data analyst... I ask questions," *The kinds of questions that cops like you are either too stupid, or too lazy to ask.* I could feel Aackster's smirk at my shoulder as my fingers dance across the holo-screens surrounding me. I tugged the images of three women from the bowels of the database and slid them into position with a practiced swipe and flip of my hand as I turned my back to the two detectives.

Again, I felt rather than saw Brasher point to the faces coming to life on the screens. "Hey, isn't that..." he exclaimed as I turned my head and caught Aackster's eyes pop open. The smirk was gone, replaced by a grimace of recognition.

"Your case, right?" I said, "Three rape-murders in the Tenderloin District." I'd seen the reports coming downstream in the data. I knew Aackster had the case and I knew with him as the lead it would be going nowhere fast. This case was a puzzle; Aackster didn't have the mind for puzzles. He barely had a mind at all.

"Yeah, our case. The third body turned up yesterday," snorted the detective sergeant. He was unhappy that I'd been poking around. "No witnesses, no DNA. It's a dead end."

I turned and looked Aackster hard in the eye, "Because you're not asking the right questions."

I pointed to the first of the three images floating in the air in front of us, "Katherine Grant, age 19. Last seen walking home through Curie Lane late on the evening of the 26th of April."

I gesture to the screen and pull out the second image, enlarging it and enhancing the still image of a young blonde woman with a pixyish hairdo, "Joanne Nash, age 17. Last seen in the area of Feynman Square at about midnight on the 16th of May."

I dip into the dataflow for the third time; I pull forward the holo-image of a young woman, a brunette this time, with large doe-like eyes, "Soledad Rodriguez, age 20. Last seen walking alone down Brahe Drive late in the evening of the 5th of June."

I pulled all three images up now and fanned them like a deck of cards across the screen. The dates of their ending floated just above each of their faces. Then I pulled up their crime scene photos and fanned them out across their ident images before continuing, "The same M.O. in all three cases. Manual strangulation. Rape kits were positive for semen, but no usable DNA found. Each killing 20-days apart, almost to the hour." I spoke as though lecturing a small child on the finer points of particle physics and trying hard to keep all my words to two syllables or less so Aackster could follow without getting a headache.

I glanced over to Brasher to see how he was doing, and I was rewarded with a bright, clear gaze lacking the perpetual haze of Aackter's slack-jawed stare.

"In order to ask relevant questions, we need to make certain assumptions. Human victims, means a human perp," I continued. "He's a non-secretor. There are no blood-type antigens in the body fluids. No DNA to find. Even the most generous estimates put non-secretors at less than 15% of the population."

"Yeah. So that takes our pool of suspects down from what? Three and a half million to just over 500,000," says Aackster with a snarl. *You're paying attention and doing math? I've underestimated you, DS Aackster.*

"Well, that's assuming he's a citizen of Ceres Station and including the female population as well." *Two can play that game, you thick-brained Dutchman.* "Once you eliminate the female population and resident aliens, you're closer to about 100,000. You are right, though. That is still a pretty big suspect pool to go swimming in."

Again I locked on to Aackter's gaze as I said," What if I could get it down to just one?"

Aackster snorted in disbelief. Brasher took a step back as though I'd just offered to change turds into tulips with a wave of my magic wand and a few secret words.

I paused for dramatic effect and continued, "With three vics we can establish continuity. Every 20 days is probative. Non-secretor is probative. The schedule suggests an insys hauler on a Marsport rounder."

Brasher finally found his voice, "Why Marsport?"

I dipped into the datastream yet again and opened up a directory, then fingered a file. Not yet. Not just yet. Let the boy have his moment. "Because the Marsport run is nine days. Nine days there and nine days back. One day dockside here for loading, and one day planetside at Marsport for off-loading. 20-days with the day on each end for the layover."

Elementary, my dear Brasher, eliminate the improbable and the possibilities that are left provide the most likely solution. Data becomes information; the information provides the answers. With the flick of a finger, I triggered the file to open and spread out my arms in a flourish as it warped into existence.

"Just one name fits all the criteria. The timeline. The physical evidence. All criteria," the image on the screen as that of a 30-ish man with a heavily pock-marked face. Beardless, with a shaved head, "His name is Martin Tannauer. An insys hauler whose runs coincide with the murders and whose medical records indicate he's a non-secretor. "

Brasher's expression was incredulous. Aackster's, true to form, showed nothing so much as disdain and disgust. About what I'd expected, "You got it down to a single name, got it solved just like that?"

"Yeah. Just like that," I returned. "There's your number one suspect, at least it ought'a be. Pick'im up. Put'im in the box and sweat'im. You know, pretend you're a cop." *Shit, I said that last bit out loud.* Bad move, I just blew any chance I had of doing this easy.

I shut my eyes and waited for Aackster's next move. I knew there'd be one. He'd look back through those, limited mental files of his for anything he might be able to use to jab it to me.

Oh, it took him a moment. A long, slow agonizing moment while I waited for the other shoe to drop.

"So why don't you come with us to pick'em up?"

That was it, then; straight for the jugular. Dig the knife in deep and give it a twist.

Boom boom.

I felt it starting. The constriction. The pounding. I put my hand on my chest and mentally I screamed, "Stop it!"

Aloud I said, as calmly as I could, "I don't do field work." The pounding grew louder, and my knees suddenly threatened to buckle beneath me. Was it my heart? My head? I could never tell. Just a pounding that left unfettered would have my whole body shaking in minutes.

Boom boom.

I find the edge of the desk and lean hard against it; I tried to will the pounding to stop by sheer mental force, but nothing. I felt the cold beads of sweat start to run down my spine.

Boom Boom.

Aacksters' there again, to pour fuel on the fire, "And why is that? I forget..."

Boom Boom.

Breathe. Stop pounding. Breathe. Breathe!

Then Aackster put his hand on my shoulder, "Not the balls for it, then?"

"Don't..." It's like a slow-motion movie. Something snapped, and I was overwhelmed by a flood of mental images.

Aackster's hand. His coffee cup. The steam still rising from it. "Ever..."

His face. His smirking, pig-ugly face, "Touch me!"

In the split-instant that followed, I saw Aackster's arm twisted up behind his back in a way that arms were never meant to twist. The coffee cup slowly orbited in the air between us. Hot sweet liquid pouring down Aackster's free arm, chest and protruding belly. I saw him swimming through the air. Doing a kind of backstroke and I though to myself, *well now, that's interesting. I wonder how he's doing that.*

Back before the hostilities between the tir'a and humanity broke out into the Great War. Back even before my days as a beat cop, I was a 19-year old Marine doing MP duty at a mud-ball base on a mud-ball world at the ass-end of the Orion Arm. Pulling shifts patrolling the perimeter in an open air jumper was grueling. The heat and humidity made the sweat pour out of you like someone had opened a spigot. Then there were these bugs, a little like mosquitoes, but big enough to stand flat-footed and screw a turkey. Any length of time spent outdoors had those little bastards trying to eat you alive.

So I'd carry along a little cooler tucked up under the front seat of my jumper. Just a few things in it to help fight off that sluggish, "God, I need a nap."

feeling you get in that kind of heat and humidity. Naps aren't encouraged for Marines standing duty. One of my staples was a small jar of strawberry preserves. A tasty little sugar shot to get the gray cells gurgling again.

As I sat in the shade of a squat, ugly tree by the side of a rarely used access road, I spotted a civilian skimmer weaving its way down the paved ribbon to the east. I hit the bubble machine and siren, and after a low-speed chase of about a quarter mile, the skimmer pulled off on the embankment, the door popped open and out tumbled a very inebriated Marine. I immediately recognized the Gunnery Sergeant's stripes and about 20-years worth of hash marks on his uniform. I could tell this wasn't going to be pleasant.

The truth is most drunks aren't that happy little inebriates. Most drunks are just mean. Marine noncoms are trained to react to lower ranks in very much the way porcupines react to wild dogs. Intimidation is ingrained in them. I fingered my Lance Corporal stripe as I approached the drunken Gunny.

"ID please, sir," I asked with as much stiff-necked professionalism as I could muster in the sweltering heat. His response was to lean forward and with, what I can only describe as unadulterated *Esprit de Corps*, puke on my shoes. He then cut loose with a full-throated belch that carried up a stench to make me think his bowels were somehow linked to Gehenna itself.

After a minute or two of bobbing and weaving, he managed to rear back against his skimmer enough to straighten up. He pulled his holo-film ID card out of his shirt pocket and flung it at me, hard. He began to spew forth the single most random series of expletives I have to this day ever heard, and the ID card bounced off my chest to land on the ground. Just short of the leavings of his earlier, more tangible, spew.

Without saying a word, I walked back to the jeep while his stream of consciousness invectives continued. *Seriously? My mother did what with a mule? Good lord, is that even physically possible?*

As expected he'd had a long list of drunken offenses, including several DUIs, a couple of misdemeanor assaults, and most recently a charge of domestic abuse. In short, the guy was not just an alcoholic jerk; he was a nasty, mean, alcoholic jerk and (my eyes lit up) driving on a suspended license.

So I reached up under the seat and extracted my little thermal container, pulled out that round jar of strawberry preserves. While the Gunny continued his, frankly unbelievable, stream of denunciations I walked back over to him carrying my jar of sweet berry goodness in one hand along with his ID, and reached into my pocket for a commemorative titanium spork I'd picked up at my last liberty.

It might have been my lack of reaction to his spew, both verbal and literal, which made him stop in mid-sentence or it might have been the amazing sight of that commemorative titanium spork that did it. I'll never be sure, but I am sure that I'd never seen anybody's eyes get quite as big as his did when I spread strawberry preserves on his ID and swallowed it.

Yeah. I ate it.

It was as if the absurdity of my actions sobered him up completely. I spun him gently around, and without resistance handcuffed him behind his back in the usual manner. He eased into the patrol jumper's back seat with a kind of resignation as I called for a tow to pick up his skimmer.

The moral of the story, kiddies?

Sometimes if you are just outrageous enough, just over the top enough, you can get away with damn near anything. Even spreading strawberry preserves on a Marine Gunnery Sergeant's holo-film ID card with a commemorative titanium spork and popping it down your gullet.

So this event, out of all the events of over nearly a half-century of living is what echoed up from

the chasms of my unconscious while I watched
Aackster, his arms flailing and singed by hot
coffee waft gracefully through the air to land on
his rather substantial buttocks. Not really sure
why. Certainly, this was one of those times I had
behaved in an outrageous manner. Certainly, I
had gotten away with it before, but this time I
suspected it would be different. A squad room
full of witnesses would be one difference; the
other would be Aackster himself.

Aackster was nothing if not vindictive. One way
or another, I was going to pay for bruising his
dignity not to mention spilling his coffee.

Brasher's reflexes were much better than I'd
have expected of someone of his size. He's
young, so I guess I shouldn't be surprised that he
was able to dodge both Aackster's bulk and the
hot coffee. Just goes to show, once again, youth is
wasted on the young.

The tympani in my chest continued as I searched
my desk for the bottle of pills I knew would take
away the drumming and thrumming before it

reached its inevitable crescendo. I barely noticed the other constables standing up to get a better view of what had happened. I slid a little on the wet floor, slick with coffee (extra light sweet) as I found the pill bottle. The drumming, thrumming, boom-booming had centered between my eyes now and the room was spinning and dark as I gulped down two (or was it three) of the capsules.

Brasher was both helping Aackster back to his feet and holding him back, keeping him from moving on me. In my state, he'd have done some damage. Those rolls of fat hid some real muscle, and I imagined they'd made him effective at beating confessions out of low life's back in the day.

"Stand down, Sergeant!" I heard the voice come from my left. The commanding tone was familiar, and I felt more than a little relief as I saw her come into the squad room. A fortyish woman, Detective Commander Sandrine (Sandy) Eason was a little better dressed than the rest of us. A little more polished; a lot more professional. As if even after all her years on this rock, she was immune to the crimson rust that wore down flesh and blood here as much as it did the iron and steel.

DC Eason put herself between us and held out her arms. She was furious, but controlling it well. No, that's an understatement. The simmering of Vesuvius in the days leading up to the destruction of Pompeii would have nothing on the constrained violence that flashed in her eyes at that moment. Sandy was the commander of our little squad of defective detectives, and the boss of us all. Most days I could also call her a friend, at that moment I wasn't all that confident of our relationship.

"Damn it!" she said through clenched teeth. "I said stand down!"

Aackster was pointing to me, and Brasher felt confident enough in the fat detective's self-control to turn him loose. He waved and wagged that finger, while I stood there and let the medication do its work. The drumming, thrumming, and hammering had subsided just about enough for me to focus on the proceedings.

From somewhere far away, I heard Aackster say, "He's assaulted a superior member."

Higher ranking, maybe, but I doubt seriously if his *member* was in any way superior.

I don't know if it was the drugs, or if that long-neglected and under-nourished kernel of common sense kicked in, but somehow I managed to stand there with Aackter glaring and fuming red-faced and didn't say a word. I didn't even burst out laughing. For once, just this once, I knew enough to let Sandy do all the talking.

"All I saw was DS Aackster, spill his coffee," she said and pointed to the upturned paper cup where it sat lost and lonely under my desk. "You should be more careful, Detective Sergeant. What with all this delicate equipment around us."

She cocked one eyebrow and looked the young Brasher in the eye and said, "What did you see Detective Constable?"

"I um... I saw..." stuttered Brasher as he looked first at the Commander, then back to his partner. Then back to the Commander. Then back to his partner. Long slow seconds ticked away, and Aackster's face grew redder and redder, at the delayed answer. ""I um... That is..." Brasher turned his eyes from them both and stared at that poor innocent coffee cup lying helpless on the floor.

Finally, he said, in a barely audible voice, "I saw DS Aackster drop his coffee cup."

Aackster pulled away from the younger man and gave him an, *Oh, no...you didn't!* evil eye.

Backed into a corner, Aacketer stood there huffing and puffing for a few more seconds before turning has back on the rest of us and stomping away. "Way to have my back, there partner," I heard him say holding his scalded arm against his chest like a wounded bird nursing its wing.

"Come'on, "Brasher said, joining him. "I'll buy you a cup'a coffee."

Again resisting the urge to get the last word I thought rather than said, *Might wanna' make that an iced coffee, Brasher.* I even resisted the almost overwhelming desire to stick my tongue out behind their backs. I don't know what came over me. Maturity taking hold like a sudden infection?

I hadn't realized I'd been so clutching the small jar of pills so tightly till I noticed my hand started to ache. I managed to pry my pre-arthritic fingers open and deposit the medication on the desk before turning back to face the tongue-lashing I knew was coming. That her admonishment would be gentle and caring, made it worse.

"Connie, you need to work on your people skills," she said. Then she spotted the medication on the corner of the desk, "Should you be gulping those like that?"

"The suppositories just didn't seem appropriate for the workplace," I answered, cursing myself inwardly for my flippancy in the face of her concern.

Sandy ignored my insubordination; we'd know each other too long for her take it to heart. She was probably the only friend I had left in the world. Hell, in the system. Probably the galaxy. I knew I was a hard man to like, but she'd known me before... before... There was that tightness again, the tremors starting in my hands. Before... I pushed *before* down deep into the dungeon where I kept it locked and chained like the fire breathing dragon it was, and let that word and the memories associated with it trail away into nothing. The shipping straps tightening on my chest loosened and the tremors subsided.

If she noticed that few seconds on the edge of madness, Sandy said nothing about it. Again, we'd known each other too long. I knew she was too good a detective *not* to have noticed, but like two evangelicals passing each other in the liquor store, we each pretended the other had seen nothing.

"What are you going to do if he goes over my head?" she said. 'What if he brings charges? He has witnesses."

"He won't," I answered. "He'd be too embarrassed to admit I put him on his ass. As for witnesses? He doesn't have a friend in the squad. Even his partner won't back him."

Realizing she was getting nowhere, she changed the subject, "You know its funny how you got it down to just one name."

I sat down, leaned back and looked up at Sandy as my fingers danced across the virtual tri-dee screens that curved around me. Once again I was the wizard, and I wove my spell with gestures and digits and data.

"Well..." I said.

"Almost as if you'd done this little exercise already."

I couldn't see my expression at that moment, but I'm sure if I could have the word *sheepish* would have sprung to mind, "The report would have

been on your com this morning, but I got...
distracted."

"Then this was all theater. Just to get Aackster's
goat?"

"No, it was about catching a killer. I started my
queries right after they called in the 3rd vic," I
said. "I had an alert on it."

I can't do field work anymore. Not since... not
since *before*. I work in my head and on my
systems. I plunge both arms elbows deep into in
the data flow and find the diamonds among the
rot and garbage. While I work the world fades
away around me and I'm there. I'm
with Tannauer. I see what he sees. I feel what he
feels. That's the part all the computers in the
world will never be able to piece together. I'm
broken. I know I'm broken. But so are people
like Tannauer. I understand broken and I can
assemble the puzzle of their minds.

Right now I know he's on
the backrun from Marsport. I can see the
cramped single crewman's berth with a hard flip

down cot. I can see the insys ship's interior. The metal bulkheads, rivets, and rust are as real to me as the cold and damp of the Station. As real as the urges that drive Tannauer and the loss and pain that eats at him. I understand him because in my own way I am him. Driven by different urges, but driven nonetheless.

"This guy won't stop. He probably survives the nine-day trip reliving the scene," I said as I imagined Tannauer getting into a cryo-tank. "He likely does cryo part of the way once he can't sate the gnawing anymore."

Sandy leans over me, and I can smell her hair as it falls to frame her face and brushes my cheek. My mind's eye pulls back again and my fingers dance and weave on the screens with a rapidity that I hardly notice anymore. The movements are peripheral. Muscle memory. Not part of the reality they create. My hands move because they know to move. My mind controls them from the lizard brain, leaving my higher functions untouched. Once again the magic manifests and the faces of two more young women materialize.

"Victims found at Marsport with the same M.O. and the timeline matches. Three days till he docks."

"You know that pair will land the collar, right?" Sandy says as she stands and steps back. I feel a little pang in my gut at that separation.

"Am I happy about that? No. Another feather in Aackster's cap," I said with just a touch of bitterness. I was resigned to the scenario playing out that way. I shrugged my shoulders at Sandy and looked across the squad room to where Aackster and Brasher stood. Back at the coffee machine.

"As long as somebody lands it," I said. *Because somebody asked the right questions.*

Sandy shook her head and put her hand on my shoulder. Hopefully, she didn't notice how I nuzzled up just slightly to meet that pressure, "What am I going to do with you?"

"Same as ya' ever did, Sandy, I said without looking up.

Then she was gone and I looked up in time to see her walk over to Aackster and Brasher. She put her hand on Aackster's shoulder just as she had done mine. There were no favorites here. Not now. Not anymore. Not since... *before*.

I turned to my screens; back to my world. The world where I'm the wizard and my magics are powerful enough to take away *any* pain. "I like the third watch," I said under my breath. "It's quiet, and they leave me alone."

-- The End

Lost Time

What do you do when you can't do what you do?

Unlike the two previous Orion the Hunter stories in this volume, *Lost Time* takes place following the events of *Vengeance is a Wheel*. We know that Orion spent three months recuperating, then six months suspended from duty. I wanted to answer the question about just *what* he was doing during that time.

From the Chronicles of Messu Sa'dish, Historian to Va'namir VII Emperor of the Tir'a People – *That one who holds a secret close and silent may be called wise, but wiser yet is that one who holds no secrets at all.*

"We do this a lot, don't we?" Federation Marshal Danni Jaheel asked her partner as she wiggled down into the webbing of her seat.

"Hmm...," responded her partner, without opening his eyes, "What?"

"This. We spend a lot of time pushing C's like this; almost as much as we spend pulling G's. A lot of time sitting in little back cabins surrounded by other people's junk."

"Hmm...," he replied. He opened his eyes and looked around soaking in the stacks of crates that filled the bulk of the five-meter square compartment. He knew that the rest of the cargo holds of the FTL freighter would be crammed full of similar crates held in place by similar webbing, but those crates didn't need to remain in a pressurized environment. The freighter's mile long bulk consisted of the tiny pressurized area that the two marshal's currently occupied, the forward flight deck where the pilot and engineer now sat and which was even smaller, and the two large cargo bays behind them. In this old style terrachian freighter the FTL engines occupied half the total length. That marvelous machinery capable of punching a hole through Einsteinian space into the realm of hyperspace where time ran at a different rate and distances were truncated.

Since the end of the Great War many of the ships of the terrachian merchant marines had been retrofitted with the more efficient hyper-drives of their former enemies, the tir'a. Not so this one. These big drives vibrated the thin walls of the freighter and the hum passing through their bodies created a soothing rhythm.

Marshal Geos Ah'rion Rassas rel Pen'atha, closed his eyes again and let that rhythm rock him back into his half-sleep. It was always like this when the travelled together. He always wanted to sleep. She always wanted to talk. Talking was never his strong suit, and t-common, the language they shared, was difficult on his half-breed vocal apparatus.

He shrugged his large frame into the webbing, working his body and trying to find a comfortable position despite his size. Ah'rion, nicknamed Orion by his far more garrulous partner, hated the stillness of these voyages between worlds. He hated the inaction. He hated the cramped quarters. He hated the ozone-laced atmosphere that bombarded his far more acute senses during these transitions. So he slept, conserving his strength for what was coming. His memories of *that* night had mercifully faded and he slept deep and dreamlessly these days; even the wide red scar that ran from his temple to his chin, no longer throbbed.

"Orion?" she said, "Did you hear me?"

By this time it was clear that she wasn't going to let him sleep, so Orion stood and stretched; his knuckles pressing in as he arched his back. His two-meter height almost matched that of the little cabin and he felt his thick braids scrape the curved bulkhead.

"Yeah," he said. "Lot of time."

The two marshals could not be more different physically or psychologically. She was little more than a meter and a half, but her physique was solid and muscular. He was a giant of his mother's race and tall even for a terrachian. Her eyes were bright green and as wide as a doe's. His almond eyes were classic tir'a with a dark iris and nearly white irises. Her hands were delicate and quick, her skin smooth and the color of coffee with cream. His three-fingered hands were large and rough, tipped with short sharp retractable claws. His skin was darker, and his arms, chest, and back were covered in the traditional tribal tattoos of a tir'a adult, called the Warrior's Journey.

They'd been together since the academy, part of the first class of *hunters* to graduate. Of that group of fourteen, half were already dead or disabled. Together these last eight years, Orion and Danni had made a formidable team. Ending or capturing more war criminals and inter-world fugitives than any other team. Even now, when the hunters of the Marshals Service numbered over 1200, these two were legends. Of all the humans Orion had known, she was the one who had shown him the most humanity.

"I said," she restated," Now that we're alone, you can tell me where you were those last six months. You know, during your suspension."

"Hmmm..." he answered back.

"Doesn't work on me, partner," she snapped back. "You know that."

"Busy," he said.

"Yeah. You mentioned that. Busy with what?

"Can't say," he said, squeezing into the webbing and shutting his eyes again.

"It's just us, Orion," she said pressing.

He opened both eyes and turned to face her. Scooting forward to the edge of the seat, he put both hands on her knees and locked his eyes with hers. In a serious voice he said, "Drop this, b'nath[2]."

"Oh, c'mon," she kept prodding. "What'dya do, sign the Official Secrets Act?"

After a few seconds of silence and holding her gaze with his, he answered only, "Hmmm." Then settled back into his seat and closed his eyes, as hers grew wide with astonishment.

II

---

[2] The tir'a rel clan tongue, a diminutive roughly translated as, "little sister."

Six months earlier...

Even through the heavy parka, Orion's ribs ached as he braved the cold Midway weather. He hurried out the walkway to the waiting autocar at the end of the ramp one arm wrapped around his waist. He never made it; a tall thin man in a long overcoat intercepted his progress. The perceptible bulge under the left arm of the coat was of particular interest to Orion, and his hand moved casually to the place normally occupied by his own blaster. He did not find the comforting roundness of its grip there. Instead, for the hundredth time since his return to Midway, he was aware of his suspension and felt a flush of anger and shame.

"Can I have a second, Marshal?" the lanky man said, raising one hand to Orion's chest. With his other hand he opened a small wallet to show his badge and ID card.

"Hmm..." replied the big marshal, as he gazed past the insignia of the Federation Intelligence Service, to study the man himself.

The agent was slightly shorter than Orion, made shorter still by a complete lack of hair. Not just bald or shaved, the officer lacked any hair whatsoever, even eyebrows. His skin was much darker even than the marshal's, a kind of deep blue-black so dark that it was almost purple. Orion had never seen a terrachian so dark.

"Brock," the man said. "Special Branch."

"I can read," said Orion and he pushed past the officer.

"I can make it worth your while, Marshal," Brock said, following close behind, his long coat swinging side-to-side and sweeping the frost from the walkway.

Orion stopped and put his hand on the roofline of the waiting vehicle. "Not a marshal," he mumbled out loud.

"I'm aware of your position. That situation is why I want to talk..."

"Hmmm..." Orion said and turned to look down his nose at the intelligence officer.

"Or I have the authority to make your suspension a lot more permanent," Brock said with an almost casual air. Orion couldn't tell if the smaller man was serious through his Cheshire cat grin.

Brock turned and headed back into the building, leaving Orion standing and looking from the autocar to where the agent stood just inside the entrance warming his hands. Orion closed his eyes and shook his head, then shut the hatch to the car and turned to walk inside.

Brock smiled as the big marshal entered. "Good choice," he said, "I'll buy you a cup of coffee."

They sat in silence for a few minutes as their coffee cooled. Orion gazed out of the big windows into the diffused light of Midway's morning. Brock took a small, flat device out of the deep pockets of his long coat. He placed it on the table between them and swiped left to activate the gadget. Orion could hear a faint buzzing in his ears.

"Jammer," Brock said. "Now we can't be scanned or recorded."

"Hmm…" said Orion.

"You are every bit as talkative as your file would indicate aren't you, Marshal?"

"Not a marshal," Orion corrected him.

"Okay. Then. I'll get right to it," said Brock. "I need you for an undercover assignment."

Orion threw back his head and laughed in Brock's face. The suddenness and harshness of the laugh stunned Brock into momentary silence. The big marshal started to stand and leave.

"Wait. Hear me out," Brock said, putting his hand on Orion's elbow. The marshal gave him a look that would have had a lesser man pull back that hand immediately, but Brock just locked Orion's dark eyes with his own and the two men seemed in momentary stasis.

"Look. I know what you're thinking," he said, as they sat back down. "Even if you weren't the biggest tir'a in known space, you've been all over the tri-dee reports for the last couple of months.

"After what happened on Rogue, you're... Well let's just say you're a face that people know."

"Hmmm..."Orion said, stroking the groove of his facial scar with one taloned finger.

"I'll give it to you straight," Brock said locking eyes again. "Half the Federation thinks you're a murderous psychopath with a badge.

"That's the man I need. Not who you are, but who people think you are."

"Your men?" asked the Marshal.

"Oh," exclaimed the agent. "So you do speak."

"When I have something to say."

Brock hung his head down and for the first time avoided Orion's piercing gaze. Waves of anger came off him like heat off a desert road. "Ten years ago, during the war... I ran an op." he began. "I was with the Military Investigative Service, then. My primary got in deep."

"His cover was blown and they tortured him for three days before we could pull him out. Hammers. Torches. What we rescued was barely human; barely alive.

"He gave them everything," despite the jammer, Brock was whispering now. "Everyone we had in their organization and others. What they didn't need they sold off to the highest bidder. A lot of people died. He was the best I had, but he's never been the same."

Brock touched the small device again and it projected a tri-dee image of two men, obviously brothers, so similar they could be twins. Both were tall, dark, well built and impeccably dressed. "Nico and Marco Cervallas. The brothers made their bones in the Great War as black marketers. That was the original investigation. After they snapped up a lot of those surplus weapons that seemed to be lying everywhere and became the biggest gunrunners in five systems.

"Somebody tipped them off ten years ago and that tip had to come from inside. Since I've been with Special Branch I've tried twice more to get at them. Both ops ended the same way. More good people died.

"The intel they got from my man back in the day they used to buy into Omak Shakti and now they're more untouchable than ever. Unlike other members of that outfit, they are flamboyant and public. We know they're close to the top of the food chain."

"Don't trust your own?" the marshal asked.

"Nope," Brock said looking up and meeting Orion's eyes again. "Not even a little bit."

"You need an unknown?" Orion asked.

"No. An unknown would take years to make it in," said Brock. "I need a 'known.' I need somebody they'll accept. Somebody like…"

"… A murderous psychopath who just lost his job," Orion completed the thought.

"Yeah," said Brock. "Somebody just exactly like that."

III

Three days pushing C's from Midway to Ceres Station, the terrachian system's main hub. From there Orion caught a convenient insys ship to Marsport and spent more days hanging in acceleration webs. Days spent going over everything Brock had briefed him with on the Cervallas brothers.

Like most terrachians, the brothers had been conscripted for military service at the beginning of the war. They reported, but attempted to leave after a few minutes. When the corporal in charge tried to stop them, Marko broke his jaw and the two men left the induction station without a word. During their unauthorized absence they assaulted another police constable who tried to arrest them, putting the young man in the hospital for more than a week. It took five constables in all to take the brothers down, and they were sent to a military prison on Luna for a month to await court-martial. Soon after, they were sentenced to five years labor. At that point a change came over them. They became model prisoners, ending up as trustees in the prison. They were out in less than two years.

After release, they quickly worked to establish themselves and their independent crew as major players in the Marsport underworld. The brothers Cervallas and their cronies were involved in robberies, arson, drugs, protection rackets, assaults and at least three murders.

As Brock indicated the brothers had begun accumulating military grade weapons at the end of the war. Most of these came from little forgotten depots like the one on Rogue; others were stolen from shipments to decommissioning stations. The success of their enterprise had brought them to the attention of Omak Shakti, and they had joined the outfit as lieutenants.

Brock wanted just three things — the location of the brother's, and by extension Omak Shakti's primary weapons cache; proof of a link between the brothers and that cache; and the name of the mole or moles who had turned three undercover operations into bloodbaths.

Outside the upscale nightclub the brothers ran as their front, Orion's hands once again felt the absence of his big blaster at his belt. He adjusted the two tir'a dueling blades he carried, moving them to the back of the wide leather belt next to the four small throwing knives he also carried there. The blades would have to be enough; the blades and his own personal weapons, he thought, as he flexed his long fingers and unsheathed his claws. He smiled and his tir'a tusks gleamed in the blue neon light, as he entered through the double doors.

A bar or a nightclub before opening time has an eerie air to it. Chairs and stools up on tables, newly swabbed floors, and empty of the beating hearts, laughter, and chatter that will fill the space to the rafters in just a few short hours. The brothers were in a circular booth in the back of the club going over the previous night's receipts. When Orion entered the two large format goons standing on either side of their table approached him with menace. Both men wore identical black suits with matching bulges in the left armpit. Their sloping brows and wide necks made them seem like caricatures of the low-level mobsters in every cheap tri-dee flick ever made. The type never changed and to Orion they were unreal. Less than true persons and more like manikins; thing one and thing two. They moved in practiced synchronization with one hand extended and the other moving to unbutton their jackets. They reached under the expensive high-quality fabric toward that left-side bulge.

Such was their confidence in their two men that the brothers hadn't even deigned to look up.

"We're closed," said Thing One.

Orion hunched his shoulders forward and lowered his head; his long braids falling to cover his face. He held up his hands as he approached, the gesture and posture meant to imply submission.

He watched and as their shoulder's relaxed and hands began to move away from their jackets, he struck. Two rapid-fire punches just above their elbows set the two men reeling back, the arms that had been reaching for their weapons hanging useless at their sides.

Orion followed that strike with a well-placed kick to the knee of Thing One that sent him to the floor, crying like a baby. Thing Two moved to bring his good arm up to throw a punch, and Orion counterpunched. He met the punch fist to fist, and bones crunched in the big terrachian's knuckles.

Orion palmed the man's face and lifted him into the air, slamming him into the hard tiles of the nightclub floor. The thug's groans were the only indicator of consciousness the man made.

Orion reached under the men's coats and removed their weapons.

He approached the brothers' table and Nico Cervallas started to rise. Marco touched his arm and said, "No, Nico. If the marshal wanted to do us harm, he'd have done so already."

Orion dropped the two compact blasters on the table between the brothers and said, "Not a marshal."

"What then?" asked Marco.

"Unemployed," replied Orion. The big half-breed hooked a thumb back over his shoulder at the two men on the ground behind him. "Seems you're hiring."

Nico, red-faced, started to get up again and again Marco tugged him back to his chair. "So this was... What? A job interview?" Marco asked.

"Hmmm..."

Marco smiled and Nico continued to fume. "You're not considering..." Nico said.

"He took out two of our best."

"They lull," said Orion.

Marco laughed out loud and even Nico cracked a smile.

Marco waved at the seat across from him and Orion sat, but with his body turned so that if the unconscious men behind him were to come around, he'd be able to move quickly. Not that they'd pose much of a threat at this point, but life in the camps had given him a healthy paranoia and a sixth sense for danger.

Right now that sixth sense was sounding off like a klaxon, despite the pleasant smiles on the faces opposite him. His hackles were up and his muscles tensed for whatever might come next.

Closer to the brothers now, he could see the slight differences that distinguished the twins. Nico's sleeveless, skin-tight tunic showed that he at least, had some work done. The small scars at his shoulders and elbows indicated the possibility of cybernetic implants for augmented strength and endurance.

Marco's more conservative attire made it difficult to see if he too had undergone enhancement, but Orion's instincts told him that one twin wouldn't have gone through such expensive and illegal procedures on his own. He'd have to watch carefully to determine just what level of augmentation they might have.

Marco presented a collected demeanor. Nico was the more nervous of the two, tapping his foot and shifting his weight in his chair. Marco's eyes never left Orion's, his gaze locked and steady. Nico's eyes flashed between the big ex-marshal and the two weapons lying on the table between them.

Orion folded his hands on his lap and relaxed his shoulders to appear as unthreatening as possible. Marco's gaze never wavered and they sat there with silence dark as a funeral scarf hanging between them. Nico's squirming continued and increased as the seconds dragged into minutes with neither his brother nor the half-breed speaking a word.

Marco said, "If you betray us, they'll never find a body." He smiled as he said that last, but the way that smile never reached those ice-blue eyes would have sent a cold shiver up most men's spine.

Orion smiled back and said, "Hmmm…"

Nico and Marco spoke together in hushed voices while Orion sat at the bar eating scrambled eggs with cheese prepared by a pretty bartender who happened to come in a little early for her shift. Marco had keyed his com and within minutes two almost identical thugs had appeared to haul away Thing One and Thing Two. Where they had been taken to, or what would be done with them when they got there, Orion did not concern himself with over much. He had no illusions about the collateral damage his mission would entail. Rumors were widespread as to how the brothers treated failed minions. None of those rumors involved a comfortable retirement. The decision to attack the pair as part of his approach had been his, but what happened to them afterward, that would be on the brothers.

Marco and Nico approached him, just as he pushed the plate away. One stood on either side, and Marco put his arm around Orion's shoulders. "We've come to an agreement, marshal," said Marco.

"Still not marshal."

"Then what?" asked Nico.

"Orion," replied the big man. "Just Orion."

"All right then, Just Orion," said Marco. "Go to the address we've sent to your com."

"To do what?" asked Orion.

"Security," responded Nico. "You'll be overseeing security for our *goods* at that location."

Orion looked from brother to brother. Each one smiled and Marco patted him on the back. "You can handle that," said Marco, "Right?"

"Hmmm..." he replied.

IV

Marsport Center was divided into a series of five concentric rings radiating out from the central hub, the port itself. The two rings closest to the hub were warehousing and manufacturing, the outer three rings were residential. The further out from the spaceport you got, the more affluent the areas became. A high-speed monorail ran out from the spaceport like the spokes of a giant wheel.

The outer ring itself was separated into four neighborhoods, with a gap of several kilometers between each. These gaps connected out to the four other domes, Marsport East, Marsport West, and Marsport North and South. These were the Marsport's rural components, reclaimed and terraformed farmland responsible for feeding the thirteen million or so inhabitants of Terra's second oldest colony.

A short rail ride brought Orion to the address on his com. It was a building in the third Central ring; just beyond the factories and warehouses, and just before the more prosperous residential precincts. Unlike some of the surrounding buildings, the squat, wide four-story building at that address was without rust or even a spec of dirt. Light spilled down from soft floodlights above the portal to illuminate the entrance. A small flowered garden flanked wide decorative stone steps leading up to the large red wooden double doors. Wood was a rarity on Mars and these doors alone were worth more than his marshal's salary would have brought him in a year. It was an obvious sign of opulence in an otherwise ordinary facade.

The effect was warm and welcoming, but as Orion walked up the steps he was well aware of the well-hidden security cameras following his every move. The door opened before he could knock.

The doorframe was filled with a large, obese, naked terrachian. In one hand, he was whipping a braided leather riding-crop in the air with some vigor. The other hand clutched the thick reddish tresses of young woman in a skin-tight leather body suit. The exposed terrachian was dragging the young woman behind him screaming incoherently all the while. His eyes were wide with something... excitement... fear... Orion couldn't tell.

"Silt," Orion said out loud. Recognizing the symptoms of the latest drug of choice to hit the Federation underbelly.

The young woman, for her part, was composed. Speaking just loud enough to be heard over the screams of her captor, she said to the assembly lining the narrow hallway behind her, "Don't just stand there. Do something!"

Orion could see other, similarly clad young women and a few men peeking around doorjambs and into the hallway to see what was happening. The men ranged in age from mid-twenties to late sixties. Most were in various states of undress.

Orion took all this in within the time it took for the naked charger to raise the whip and aim it at the tall ex-marshal's head. Before the strop of the leather could reach his face, Orion had reached up and grabbed the crop. The braided rawhide stung his palm instead of the flesh of his cheek.

Orion's claws sprung and it was by a force of will he resisted tearing at the crazed man's throat. Instead, holding the riding-crop in one hand, he struck the man center of his chest with the heel of his other palm, taking care not to rip into fat man's flesh.

The terrachian staggered back, and a twist of Orion's wrist sent the riding crop into the air. His grip on the auburn haired woman at his feet did not release as easily, the wild mane now so entwined between the wild man's fingers he couldn't release it if he'd wanted to.

Drawing one of his twin assu khtra, the tir'a dueling blade carried by all adults of his race, Orion slashed through the tangled web, separating the of hair from the man's grip without separating the man's fingers from his hand. The woman leapt up and ran back to the arms of one of the waiting watchers, while the fat terrachian looked at the furry mass still clutched in his hand in wonder. Orion re-sheathed the blade with a practiced flip and prepared to face what came next open handed.

The human cast aside the red-gold threads and raised both fists above his head. He charged Orion, eyes now mad with unredeemable rage. As though he were a child whose favorite toy had been broken. Orion punched the man full in the center of his face. Bone shattered and blood sprayed behind the edges of the massive knuckles.

The fat man stopped, shook his head violently and sneezed blood into his hands. A split second later, he resumed his charge. This time, Orion slipped beside the terrachian, no mean feat given their combined bulk and the narrowness of the hallway. Once at the man's back, he reached around and thrust his arm between the rolls of fat that hid the human's neck. With his other arm, he formed a triangle of muscle enveloping the throat. The crook of the elbow at point of the man's Adam's Apple so not to crush the windpipe, Orion applied pressure using his forearm and biceps to close off the jugular veins and interrupt the blood flow to the brain. Within seconds the terrachian fell unconscious to the floor, Orion sliding down to sit behind him.

"You didn't kill him, did you?" came a voice from behind him.

Orion released the stupefied human and stood to face the speaker. What he saw as he reached his feet was a tall slender Asian woman of almost indeterminate age. She wore a silk jacket with an intricate brocade design in red and gold. Broad pantaloons of a similar color, but without the intricate needlework covered her thighs to mid calf, and black leather lace-up boots with tall spiked heels completed the outfit. She was cradling the red-haired captive against her like a child, stroking the cropped hair and hushing her with soothing cooing sounds. "There, there," she said to the crying girl. "You handled it well. No panic."

Turning her gaze back on the half-breed she restated, "You didn't, did you? Kill him, I mean. You didn't kill him?"

Once again adopting the unspoken language of the terrachians, Orion shook his head.

"Good. When he's not cooked on silt, he's one of our best clients," she responded between making shushing noises to the girl.

She passed the girl to two other young women at her right elbow, and turned her full attention to the big ex-marshal. "I'm sorry, it's unusual for things to be so... chaotic... around here."

The woman extended her hand in greeting and bowed, "I'm Dr. Maureen Hikama. This is my clinic."

Orion looked down the hallway at the doors, now shut, where he had seen half-naked men and women peeking around just moments before. "Clinic?" He said, repeating the word as if he couldn't believe he had heard it.

"Yes, Clinic," she said annoyed at his tone. "We are a licensed therapeutic cooperative. A private club for men and woman to find ways to relieve the stress of everyday life through role play and fantasy."

He gave her a sideways look. "Sex club?"

"Definitely not," she snorted. "Sex for hire is forbidden on Mars. We are a legal and licensed business. We pay taxes. I hold degrees in psychology and sociology from the University of Luna and I am a registered therapist."

Money laundering, he thought to himself. Aloud he said, "Cash business?"

"As you can imagine, many of our clients wouldn't like to leave a record of their... proclivities... so yes. Yes, we are a cash business. That... as they say... is where you come in."

While they spoke, they walked down the hallway toward the back of the house. They passed a door that hadn't been closed quite all the way; Orion glimpsed a middle-aged man strapped into an x-shaped framework with cushioned manacles. Two young women, wearing little more than thongs, were tickling him with feather dusters.

"The brothers..." Orion began.

She cut him off, "Yes, yes. They said they'd be sending someone." Bending in close she whispered, "We don't mention them here. Never here; never."

They entered a large office and she motioned him to the antique chair that faced an ornate, and also antique, desk while she took her own seat. "Your duties will include providing security during the twice-daily credit transfers. While the Clinic itself is quite legal, the banks are... hesitant... for various reasons of compliance to hold our money in a standard account. We make deposits in person to a security box within the bank.

"Your job is to make sure the deposits are made without incident."

"Hmmm..."

"There are occasional... very occasional... scenarios like the one at the door today which you might also be called upon to deal with."

"Bouncer?" he asked.

"Security," she replied smiling. "You have an apartment on the fourth floor. You're expected to be on site unless you give me sufficient notice to arrange a temporary replacement. Let us know of any special needs you might have and we'll tend to them."

She began to stand in a dismissive way and then seemed to catch a wild thought. "Dietary needs... I meant," she said looking him up and down. "Any special *dietary* needs."

The fourth floor "apartment," as it turned out, was a four-meter by three-meter, freestanding concrete bunker of a building set in the middle of the large flat roof. Big, narrow windows faced the front of the building, with a wide short door set into the center of the facade.

Orion shut the staircase door and crossed the stone covered roof to the little bunker. He ducked under the low header and entered the single Spartan room. There was a couch, a large tabletop surface that was meant as a desk and dining table, a hammock, and a security wall. The entire back of the small building was covered with tri-dee security screens; each one showing a different part of the Clinic. He noticed that the interior *playrooms* and the Dr.'s private office were absent from the security net.

"Complicated," he said to the empty room. He had seen a similar set of security monitors peeking from behind a screen in Hikama's office.

Every coming and going in the Clinic was monitored, checked, crosschecked, and cataloged. Communicating with Brock would be, "Complicated," he muttered again.

Orion put down his go bag and walked out on to the flat gravel rooftop to watch the carbon-dioxide snowfall against the outer dome.

He stood there for several minutes turning over the problem of getting messages to his handler without being seen. His sharp hearing caught a noise from the third-floor stairwell, and he crouched bringing both his tir'a dueling blades to the ready.

The door to the lower floors opened and in the dim light of dusk Orion could see red-gold hair come peaking around its edge. He sheathed his knives and crossed to the entrance. Wrapping his large three-fingered hand around the small, thin wrist that came next into view, he tugged the young woman into the dying light of the rooftop.

She stood to just below his chin, and her eyes got very wide as she looked up at his face, but she didn't scream. She was very composed for someone face-to-face with a giant tir'a ex-marshal.

He sized her up and recognized her as the girl he had rescued in the hallway earlier in the day. "What?" he said.

"I…" she stammered, "That is… um… I wanted to thank you."

"Hmmm…"

She reached up and touched his face pulling her body close to his. "To show my appreciation."

Her touch was so much like that other touch, that touch that was lost to him now. It brought a flood of feelings, but not the ones she had expected. The hurt and the guilt from the deaths he had caused, her death. It was all too raw; the wound still seeping.

He took her hand and removed it from his face. "No," he said.

She jerked back her hand as it had taken an electric shock. Angered clouded her bright blue eyes, "I'm not a whore, you know."

Before she could stomp away, Orion put one hand on her shoulder and cupped her chin with his other. Holding her eyes with his, he said, "Someone was lost to me."

Her expression went blank as she looked into the almond-shaped inside out eyes of the half-breed. "Someone important."

The redhead flipped her hair back coyly and smiled. "I can make you forget her."

The closeness of her body, the softness, and the scent of her tempted for an instant, but the pain returned. Like an unseen hand it squeezed his heart. "Not even you."

V

The next two months passed at an excruciating pace. Twice a day, Orion made the trip down to the Doctor's office to pick up the receipts; 10AM and 4PM each day. The doctor would count the receipts into a lock box, then Orion would take the box in an autocar to the bank. The reverse would happen there, the bank manager would recount the receipts and they'd go into the vault.

Other than that, Orion didn't leave the confines of the house. Meals were brought up to him by kitchen staff, and he often spotted the redhead as he made his way from the Doctor's office with the deposits. That was the closest thing to a friendly face he had seen in weeks. He was a virtual prisoner in the rooftop bunker; isolated and alone with nothing more than his thoughts to keep him company.

It was just over nine weeks into his new employment, when Orion received the signal. A sharp sudden pain shot through his inner forearm deep into the Martian night. Speedy Phobos was rising in the west for the second time as he rolled out of the hammock and took a seat at the table in the middle of the room.

Stretching out his arm on the table, he used one of his small throwing knives to make a small incision into the skin, just below the inside curve of his elbow. Pinching the flesh made grey-green blood ooze from the edges of the wound, and something else came bobbing to the surface.

Weirwan technology was organic, and untraceable in the body. The little tracker, no larger than a grain of rice had been implanted just after Orion's meeting with Brock. Now it buzzed and vibrated on the tabletop, signaling Brock's readiness to meet.

Orion wiped down the table, cleaned his knife and used the butt end of the handle to crush the signaling device. Little more than dust remained of the tiny machine when he had finished grinding.

He rose up and stretched his inhuman hearing to its limits, checking the house below for any sounds of life. There were none. The clinic was not a twenty-four hour operation, closing for a few hours each night to clean and reset the toys.

His own movements had been silent, and his night vision allowed him to accomplish the removal and destruction of the tracer in almost complete darkness. He knew he was unobserved.

Fishing into his go bag, he took out a light absorbing skin-tight tunic and leggings and changed. He added heavy black yark-hide gloves, with the fingertips cut away to allow the use of his claws. With the hood pulled tight the center of his face and the tips of his fingers were visible as lighter shadows against the darkness. The rest of him was shadow, though his night vision membrane gave his eyes a ghostly blue-green glow.

Even in the habitat ring with its gravity grid, the pull of the Martian surface was less than 80% of Terran normal. Combined with the leaping ability inherited from his mother's people, Orion would have had no trouble dropping to the ground from the third-floor roof. The risk of being seen was to great moving that way through the neighborhood below. Even at this time of night, someone could be watching, waiting, or even just walking their dog in the pale moonlight now washing the building's façade.

Instead the big man had plotted another course, across the rooftops, hopeful that none of the buildings between his concrete aerie and the designated meeting place would be alive this time of night. Unable to predict just where the brothers might station the ex-marshal, Brock and Orion had arranged to meet three kilometers due south of whatever position the tracer showed him at when the signal was activated.

Orion stepped to the southern edge of the building and mentally measured the distance to the adjacent roof; just over 15 meters, as near as he could tell and slightly lower. It would be a near thing, even with the gifts of his tir'a heritage; 15 meters would be at the edge of his capabilities. Time for a leap of faith.

Drawing back from the lip he sprinted to the waist-high barrier and launched himself into the night like an arrow. He could tell before he'd reached the half-way point that he'd fall short. Stretching out his long arms, he extended his claws and caught the narrow edge of that opposing canopy. His claws digging in like a grappling hook.

In one smooth motion, he swung his body around, and flipped backwards up, landing with meager of scraping sounds as his boots skidded on the loose gravel that covered the flat surface. He crouched like that for a full minutes, as his sense reached out around him searching for any hint of occupants stirring below. He took control of his panting, subduing his breathing and calming his nerves. He looked up to see that Phobos had neared the completion of its ride across the night.

Moving with incredible stealth Orion peered over to the next rooftop and was relieved to see that the second building was just over half the distance. Again came the leap into the inky blackness of the night, and the soft thud of touching down on the opposite roof.

Orion continued this pattern of leaping, stopping, listening, and leaping again more than a dozen times as he headed to the blind meeting site. He covered the three-kilometer run in just over an hour.

The last jump brought him onto the much lower rooftop of a light industrial factory. The well-lit perimeter indicated that whatever widgets the little facility was churning out, they churned in three shifts. Orion knew there was a good chance that the factory would be automated, and the noise from the machinery would cover his landing. Still, he could feel the tension rising from the pit of his stomach as he made that last jump.

Orion drew the *assu khtra* as he flipped through the air while his feet were still a few centimeters above the roof. By the time he crouched low crouched low in the shadows, he was alert and ready for an attack. A heightened awareness told him that something shared his rooftop perch.

"You're late," came a whispered voice from the shadows to his left.

"Hmmm," he answered and sheathed the dueling blades. "Not that easy to sneak up on."

"I'm stealthy," Brock said. He stepped out of a patch of darkness like shedding a cloak, the Cheshire cat grin once more in place.

Orion knew this was more than stealth. His night vision should have picked up the outline of the agent despite the darkness, and his hearing should have detected the hairless man's breathing. No. Something more than stealth was at work here. A personal cloaking device? Outlawed for civilian use, such an instrument might be a very handy thing for a Special Branch operative to keep in his personal toolbox.

"Why the meeting?" Orion asked. "Why now?"

"They're going to be moving you soon," said Brock. "We think back to the nightclub, but we can't be sure."

"How do you know they're moving me at all?"

"We've been applying pressure to the organization. Picking off low-level operators and henchmen. We've also embargoed the spaceport and prevented any known felons from entering."

Orion's expression showed concern, "Won't they suspect?"

"Crims commit crimes," he said flashing that big grin again. "It's what they do. All these guys have side jobs they're working, and we've done this before. The brothers see it as a cost of doing business. They know we can't maintain it for long.

"They're not going to leave a valuable resource like you sitting in a whore house while they're short handed."

"So they'll move me," Orion said, nodding.

"Yes. We expect within the next few days. Probab from prosecution by the end of the week."

"Then what?"

"Then keep your eyes open," Brock said.

Orion eyed the operative suspiciously, "You didn't call me out just to tell me that."

"No. There's more," Brock said averting his eyes. "The local LEOs[3] are aware you are on Mars. Moving you from their legitimate operations to their less savory ones will put you in much greater danger. Nobody knows your true status here but me. While you're undercover you

---

[3] Law Enforcement Officers.

operate in a state of grace. For anything short of murder that you need to do to maintain your cover, you're protected... but..."

"But the LEOs don't know that," Orion answered for him.

"Given your reputation, if you're found committing a crime, they'll shoot you on sight," Brock finished. "I can give you this one last chance to pull out. After this..."

Orion did not answer but shook his head. Brock took his meaning, "In for a penny, in for pound, eh?"

"Hmmm."

"Then just time to upgrade your wetware," the agent said as he pulled out an inoculator. "This one will act as a recorder, but it can be detected if you know what you're looking for. Activate it when you have them on the weapons by pinching it."

Orion rolled up his sleeve and Brock shot the tiny transceiver deep into the muscle. "You might feel some pain when it's active. Like a burning, but that's normal."

The return trip to the concrete aerie was much quicker and even the high jump back to the roof of the Clinic seemed easier. Dawn was breaking and light danced on the carbon-dioxide snow crystals, shining like tiny diamonds on the dome as he stood outside the little rooftop building. Brock's words echoed for him, 'They'd just shoot you on sight."

He laid down in the hammock to grab what sleep he could, but those words made for a fitful and uneasy nap.

VI

Brock's prediction was, if anything, a little slow off the mark. Not so much the end of the week, as the end of the day. Just before the second bank trip that day, one of the neckless thugs from Orion's first meeting with the brothers showed up at the Clinic to let him know he was expected at the nightclub that evening, and not to expect to return. He could hear Doctor Hakima breathe a deep sigh of relief as he made his way, go-bag in hand, out the door. From the corner of his eye, he spotted the redheaded girl and had a momentary pang of regret.

Over the next couple of months Orion got an education in the Martian underworld. Payoffs, protection, prostitution and drugs – the brothers had a hand in it all. The scale of their operation was more than a little overwhelming. Eight weeks in, Orion was put to work shadowing Nico on the daily collection runs. Most of the collections were handled by foot soldiers in the organization, but for large gambling and protection debts, or those where there had been trouble in the past, Nico liked to take a personal hand.

Nico's reputation was no small matter, he lacked any compunction whatsoever when it came to breaking bones to make his point and his temper was well known. With Orion in tow as backup, the scent of fear when they walked up to a target was palpable. This meant for very smooth sailing and collections were at an all time high within a few weeks. Marco was very pleased with the operations, but Orion could see that Nico was edgy, restless, and looking for an excuse to inflict pain.

The opportunity came sooner rather than later. Nico and Orion sent to collect a gambling debt from a wealthy industrialist that had lost big at one of the backroom high-stakes card games the bothers organized after hours at the club. He'd been down 40,000 credits by the end of the night, and Marco had given him 48-hours to make good. His time was up.

Orion sensed trouble the minute they entered the office. All 300-pounds of ostentatious rich man sat overflowing a leather chair the size of a small sofa behind an ornate wooden desk that must have weighed more than a ton. A clear show of wealth on a world where wood and leather were scarce. Every other part of him also screamed his standing. From a hideously orange colored coif and bright colored shirt, to the diamond earring and jeweled watch he wore.

Wealth without constraint, screaming, "Look at me. I am somebody."

Standing two to either side of the desk were four large robust men with a military bearing. Orion recognized their neck tattoos from the files that Brock had provided for him to study, they were from the LGMs. While the brothers might have the largest crew on Mars, they were not the only game in town. The *Little Green Men*, or LGMs, were a well-established gang whose drug and prostitution operations were second only to Nico and Marco's.

"What's this, Ondine," asked Nico, smiling between clenched teeth. "A welcoming committee?"

"It occurred to me," said the fat man, "That it might be cheaper to hire some muscle than pay you and your cheating-ass brother. I got them for ten grand, so I get to pocket the other thirty."

Nico laughed, "Ten thousand? They'd have done it for half. You got ripped fat man."

Orion fingered one of the small throwing blades at his back, and watched the eyes and the shoulders of the LGM soldiers. It was apparent that at least two were carrying blasters in shoulder holsters, and equally apparent which of the four men was primed to move first. Orion turned his eyes on that man. That was the leader, the alpha. None of the others would move until he did. That was a mistake. Better armed and two against four; they might have had a chance striking in concert.

A slight twitch, what gamblers call a tell, alerted Orion to the other man's intent, even before his hand moved under the loose tunic he wore. Before that hand got half way to the opening, one of Orion's small, double-edged blades was embedded at the point of that shoulder, as if it had sprouted from within. The blade separated the ball from the socket.

By the time Nico's fist smashed the face of the thug nearest him, a second blade was already in the air. That man went down hard, his face a mass of blood and broken flesh. That blade found its mark through a tunic, piercing the third thug's hand and pinning it to his ribs as he reached for his weapon.

Orion sprang ahead of Nico and punched the last of the four bodyguards in the throat, dropping him to his knees spitting blood, where Nico kicked him in the side of the face, sending him sprawling. The first gangster was clutching at his shoulder trying to pull out the blade when Orion put the heel of his palm against the terrachian's chin and sent him to slumber.

The twin backhanded the last man standing and Orion could hear the bones of the jaw shatter at the blow. He remembered the small surgical scars he had seen at their first meeting, and was now certain that illegal implants augmented Nico's strength.

It was over in seconds. Less time than it took for the fat man to open the drawer of his desk and reach for the small needler he had concealed there. Another flash, and Ondine screamed as a third steel needle pinned his hand to the top of the desk.

Nico's eyes flashed as he reached across the desk and pulled out the blade. He tossed it over his shoulder in Orion's general direction. The half-breed sidestepped and caught the blade in the air. Nico barely noticed the feat as he drug the fat man's carcass across the desk and onto the floor.

Ripping off a piece the loudly colored shirt, Nico wadded it up and stuffed it into the screaming maw. He bent down low till he was practically nose-to-nose with the hysterical man and said, "A couple of things, fat man..."

Standing, Nico put his foot on the man's chest, pushing down hard enough to interfere with his already ragged breathing. "Nobody welches on me and my brother and..."

He kicked Ondine hard in the side, "We! Don't! Cheat!" Each word reinforced by another kick.

Nico reached back onto the desk and grabbed a large pair of shears, holding them like a knife and drawing them back over his head. At this point, Orion stepped forward and grabbed that arm, stopping the downward blow that would have killed Ondine.

Nico's face became a mask of rage and foam flew from his lips. Orion could actually feel the servos augmenting Nico's strength vibrate and despite the marshal's own considerable power, it took both hands to hold back that deathblow.

After a second of struggle, Orion said, "Dead men don't pay."

The wildness abated from Nico's eyes, without ever fading entirely, but he relented. "You're right," he said blinking as he dropped his arm.

Bending down to Ondine's face once again, he shifted the scissors in his hand and clamped them lightly on the fat man's ear. "You have the money here?"

Ondine's nod was barely perceptible, but clear. Nico increased the pressure of the blades just a hair, "Where?"

Ondine's eyes cut to the wall, and Nico stood him up, keeping the scissors in place the whole time, and marched him in the direction indicated. A quick retinal scan revealed a small wall safe and inside were stacks of credits.

While Nico continued to control Ondine, Orion reached in and counted out 40 thousand. When Nico reached in to take a bit extra, Orion closed the opening. "Not thieves."

Groans were coming from the men on the floor as they started to regain consciousness. Nico still had Ondine's ear gripped with the scissors as he said, "Still. A little something extra for our trouble, eh?"

Even with Orion's speed he didn't have time to react as Nico snapped shut the shears and sent the diamond-studded earlobe flipping into the palm of his free hand.

Ondine screamed again and fell to the floor with tears streaming down his face. He was still screaming through the gag as they left the office

and made their way down through the rear exit
and onto the street.

Nico rolled his neck and it popped loudly, "Now
that was fun. I needed that. They never last long
enough, though. Don't you think?"

"Hmmm."

"Yeah, I suppose you're right. Still..." Nico said.
"There is one more thing."

Nico was not a tall man, not as tall as Orion. So as
they walked side-by-side, it was easy to slip back
into Orion's blind spot, just behind his field of
vision. For once the half-breed's sense for danger
failed him and he didn't see the blow coming till
it struck him square in the jaw, just under the
chin. Orion fell hard into a stack of trashcans, the
brick wall behind them scraping his shoulder
raw.

Nico's smiling face was the last thing he saw that
night before he slipped into the expanse, "Don't
ever touch me again, or I'll kill you," he said
calmly.

VII

A green and purple bruise discolored the side of Orion's face when he entered the club later that night. He was late for his shift on the door, but seeing his mood the other members of the brothers' crew took pains to take no notice.

Marco did notice and approached the ex-marshal, "You're late."

"Hmmm."

"You're never late," Marco observed. He tugged Orion's chin to the side to get a better light on the bruise and his eyes cut to where his brother stood at the bar. "He did this?"

"Hmmm."

"I got the gist of what happened with Ondine. You did well, I'll see to it you're compensated for that."

Marco pointed to the bruise and said, "And this."

"Hmmm."

Marco began to walk away, but turned back and said, "I know Nico can be… impulsive, but he's still my brother. I'd be upset if anything happened to him; anything sharp for example. You understand that right?"

"Hmmm."

Marco drew close to Orion, their chests practically touching, "I need to hear you say it."

Orion's eyes narrowed, "I understand."

"Good. Good," Marco said smiling. He clapped Orion on the shoulder and turned to join Nico at the bar.

Just as the club was shutting down and the bartender and waitresses were putting the chairs and stool up on tables for the night, a last minute caller was shuffled toward the back office. He was a small nondescript man with a round florid face in an immaculate bespoke suit complete with leather gloves. Marco greeted him with a curt bow and even Nico seemed deferential.

Orion searched the corners of his mind for a description in the files that Brock had given him that might match the little man. Only one name came to mind, *Debiers*.

That one of Omak Shakti's top men was making a personal visit to the club was significant. The Brothers and Debiers chatted like old friends and made their way back to the main office. Orion knew that he had to find a way to be privy to their discussions.

With his clawed finger he removed the tiny weirwan listening device from his forearm and wiped away the green-gray ooze the deed left behind. He activated the device and moved down the corridor behind the men and into range. The trio entered the office and through the crack in the door as it closed he fired off the tiny pellet with his thumb and forefinger. The device shot well into the room beyond and rolled under the desk against the far wall. He barely caught sight of it as the door snapped shut.

A desperate move and half a plan, he'd still have to recover the mechanism at some point after the meeting. Recover it from an office that stayed well locked and guarded when not occupied by one or both of the brothers. Recover it without either of them being the wiser. Inwardly he shrugged; he'd burn that bridge when he came to it.

It was not unusual for the wait staff and security to stay for several hours after closing. There was the nightly back room card game and clean up to handle. So Orion knew his continued presence in the club would raise no eyebrows. He sat at the end of the bar where he'd be facing that locked door and nursed an ale.

Less than an hour later, Debiers and the brothers exited the office, but Marco did not turn and flip the locks. Instead he called out to one of the waitresses, "Chyna, clean up in there, and bring us fresh drinks to the game room."

Debiers didn't follow the brothers upstairs, but nodded to them then whispered something to

Marco as he shot a sideways glance at Orion before ducking out the back door and into a waiting autocar. Marco laughed at whatever remark Debiers had made, and he and Nico climbed up to join the games of chance that would go on till well past dawn.

Orion watched Chyna grab an empty tray and head for the open door to the office and his half-plan grew to completion. Following behind, he stopped when the neckless thug guarding the door put out his hand just short of touching Orion's chest. The man cocked his head and raised his brows at the half-breed, without saying a word. Orion responded by cutting his eyes to Chyna, who was now bending over the room's short table and collecting glasses onto her tray. Then he winked at the guard.

A knowing smile crossed the man's face and he gave his head a quick tilt of approval as he removed his hand and let Orion proceed into the room.

Even on the hard tile floors of the club, Orion made barely a sound as he moved. On the plush carpet of the office floors, he was quiet as a cat. Creeping up on Chyna as she was occupied with clearing the table, he cleared his throat.

Startled, the young woman straightened up too quickly and almost lost the tray, glasses clinking as she struggled to maintain her balance. She might have succeeded, too, but as Orion reached out to steady her, he knocked the tray away as if by accident. Sending tray, glasses, ice and other contents shooting across the floor some rolling as far as the desk against the back wall.

"Sorry," he said, bending down to help her recover the tumbled tumblers. Orion could hear no-neck laughing in the hallway as he reached under the desk the desk and palmed the listening device. "Wanted to ask to walk you to the tube stop. Didn't mean to startle."

"It's okay," she said. "And I appreciate the offer, but I don't think my wife would approve."

"Hmmm."

They left the office and the guard pulled shut the door and locked it. "Smooth," he said as Orion passed him in the hall. Orion just smiled and pocketed the little listening device.

VII

The Raczkowski Hotel was comfortable and close to the club, less than a five-minute walk. That's why the brothers had bought it and carved out the top three floors for the use of their crew. For Orion, that presented some of the same problems as the Clinic's concrete fourth floor bunker, and some new ones.

Unlike his former aerie, he was not on the top floor and even if he had been, taller buildings surrounded "The R," as the gang referred to it. So a rooftop freerun was not in the cards.

At each of the subsequent meetings after that first, Brock and Orion had arranged their next rendezvous. It wasn't that hard to slip Nico for a few hours when they were making collections. Nico had his own side jobs and would often ditch Orion, sending him back to the club on his own.

They were not scheduled to meet again for two more nights, and Orion had no way of knowing how time sensitive the information on the recorder might be. He'd have to risk the play back himself.

Back in his suite, he removed the rice-grain sized device and held it to his ear. It was one thing to be told that weirwan technology was organic, it's how these devices became invisible within his body. It was quite another to experience how his natural warmth affected the active mechanism as he held it to his ear.

He could feel minuscule tendrils half the thicknesses of the thinnest human hair extrude from the capsule. The cilia shot into the ear canal and pulled the device away from his fingertip, crawling deep into the opening.

The first experience was pain. Excruciating pain, accompanied by bright flashes of light and the sound of a siren exploding inside his head. Now he understood. It was not a mechanism. Not a device, it was a living thing; an animal that had been dormant in his body, but was now living in his skull.

Orion doubled over and fell to the floor, as the Lilliputian creature reached the eardrum and the tendrils connected to his sensitive nerves. He rolled to his back and the scene of the brothers' office replaced the room around him. Not an image, not even tri-dee, but a memory. A shared experience broadcast directly into his brain by the alien presence that now inhabited his mind.

Within a few seconds he experienced the whole of the meeting with Debiers. He had it all. Times, dates, the rendezvous points... all of it.

Its memory cargo shifted, Orion felt a shiver run down his spine as the creature exited his ear. Sitting up, he could see blood and other fluids in a small pool on the carpet. The life form was dissolving before his eyes and soon nothing but a gooey stain was left to indicate it had existed at all.

Orion rose up on his hands and knees and was hit with violent and sudden nausea. He retched and vomited staggering to his feet using the wall as support.

As unpleasant as all that was, Orion did not have time to wait till the tornado in his stomach and hurricane in his head abated. In less than two hours the brothers and the guns would be together in the same place. One chance to get them all, so he'd have to risk the dead drop and hope the brothers were too busy getting ready for their shipment to be keeping too close an eye on him.

Brock had arranged the dead drop in a nearby green space and planted an encrypted com unit adhered to the underside of a bench there. Getting out of *The R* posed little problem, and in less than half an hour he had recovered the unit and signaled Brock to meet.

The park was just beginning to fill with lunchtime visitors, when Orion spotted the dark man approaching. Before he'd crossed half the distance between them Brock turned and made for the opposite end of the park. Keeping the top of the agent's baldpate in sight, Orion followed and they crossed out of the green space and through a maintenance door into a small autocar parking facility half a kilometer south.

Orion approached the third floor charging bay as Brock stepped out of the shadows to meet him. "Your tradecraft is for shit, marshal."

"Wasn't followed," Orion replied. "And still not a marshal."

"I don't think you were," Brock said. "But I was. Right from our field ops office and that means somebody either saw you signal me or was monitoring that frequency.

"I was able to shake my tail, but it confirms that there's a mole in my operation. Now what was so urgent?"

"The brothers are moving merchandise tonight. In a little over an hour."

Orion retold his trick with the recording device, and what he'd learned during the playback. "I'm not surprised it had that affect. The mechanism was keyed to my genetic signature. Using it like that could have killed you."

"Hmmm."

"Do we know how many men they'll have with them?

"No."

"Do we know who the buyers are?"

"No."

"So we have a time and place. We know my sections out as far as organizing backup, and I don't trust the locals as far as I can throw a starship. That leaves just us."

"Just two? Asked Orion.

We'll have to hope that the brothers want to keep the party small for security, and we'll have the element of surprise on our side," there came that Cheshire Cat grin again and Brock reached under his coat. "I brought you a little something,"

He held out the bundle to Orion and the half-breed could see it was his service weapon and gun belt; the proverbial big gun. The one he'd been pining for all these months. Orion bared his tusks and jutted his head upwards in a tir'a smile.

"I was hoping for this news and thought you might need it," said the agent.

Orion strapped on the weapon and pulled his coat around it for concealment. Mars wasn't some frontier world where open carry was common. It was civilized and flaunting such a piece as his would draw undue attention.

"This way," the agent indicated and Orion could see a waiting autocar just ahead. "Air gapped and off network. Untraceable, even by my own people; paranoia, like stealth, comes in handy in this business."

Brock took the controls and used the override commands to switch to manual. They left the garage by way of a narrow back alley cloaked in the shadows of the tall buildings surrounding it.

"I always suspected it was here, right under our nose," Brock said as they approached the warehouse ring nearest the port. "To be able to shift so much on and off world, it had to be closest to the port. With thousands of warehouses and containers in this area, there was just no way to pin it down."

Brock removed two large dark visors from his pockets and unfolded them. He put one on and handed the other to Orion, but he waved them off. "I don't need..." he began to say.

"Not just night vision. They'll give you a heads up for my sensor array." Orion raised an eyebrow at the agent. "In my coat... a sensor web. Out here it's blocked, but once inside it'll help us pinpoint the players and might keep us from shooting each other. Coms are built in."

Orion put on the visor and could see what Brock meant. The heads up display gave him speed and distance as they covered the ground to the warehouse and identified Brock as a friendly, even when a low wall separated them.

The warehouse was a long, low, two-story affair. Floodlights illuminated the open parking lot in the front, and Orion could see at least two men patrolling the edge of the roof. He pointed first to the men, then to himself, then back to the men. Brock nodded in agreement to the unspoken plan.

Silent as a grave, Orion circled around away from the floodlights and to the side of other building furthest away from the rooftop guards. With a powerful leap, he just managed to dig his claws into the lip of the roof and pull himself up. Creeping low, he approached behind the two terrachians unseen and unheard.

The immediate problem was that they were too far apart or too close; too far to attack at the same time and too close to attack one without alerting the other. Orion needed a strategy to force them in one direction or the other. He decided that separation was the best choice and crept back to the farthest edge of the roof to enlist Brock's help.

He thumbed his com and explained his plan to Brock. The men synchronized their movements and shifted to opposite sides of the building. On cue, each made a soft scraping noise one from above, and one from below.

The two guards separated and went to check for intruders. Orion used one of the roof's big air ducts as cover and grabbed the first man in the same blood choke he'd used on the fat man at the Clinic. Within seconds he was lowering the unconscious thug to the ground, and skirting around to the other side of the roof where Brock's distraction had carried the other thug.

The second guard was just a little more alert, and started to turn as Orion approached him from behind. A rapid-fire punch to the throat ensured he would raise no alarm and Orion applied the same chokehold to send that man to slumber as well.

With both men unconscious Orion used their belts and shoelaces to tie them up and cut strips from their tunics to make gags. Then he signaled the all clear to Brock and crawled up to the large skylight for a view inside.

Thumbing his com he told Brock, "Four men on the catwalk just below me. Three more by the loading dock. Large covered truck loading crates."

"Any sign of the brothers?"

"Them and two others watching the crates load."

"Can you take the four on the catwalk?"

Orion scanned the cavernous room below and his eyes fell on a large winch and hook hanging down from the ceiling about three meters to the left of the skylight. "Yes."

"Watch for my cue," said Brock.

"What?"

"You'll know it when you see it."

Less than two minutes later, Brock entered through the big double doors and announced, "You're all under arrest!"

The four men on the catwalk turned their weapons on him and started firing. Orion kicked through the skylight, sending glass shards falling into the center of the room and leapt for the hook, drawing his pistol.

Catching the chain with his free hand and locking his foot into the hook, Orion swung past the four shooters on the catwalk and squeeze four shots from his big blaster. The four men went down in sequence. Like dominos falling one after the other, dropping from the catwalk to spill their blood on the concrete floor, four meters below.

Orion had assumed Brock to be a dead man after that entrance, but when he turned his attention to the door, he saw the agent standing there feet spread wide with a lightning gun in each hand and blasts that should have torn him apart curving around his body. "PPF," a shocked Orion said out loud. Such a personal protection field wouldn't hold out long and it had its own vulnerabilities. The brothers knew this, and Nico broke from the pack to charge Brock while the agent reloaded. His shield wouldn't hold against a kinetic attack and with Nico's enhanced strength, he could tear the agent apart with his bare hands.

Orion kicked off the hook and twisted his body into a diving tackle, bull-dogging the younger brother into the concrete floor.

Brock was moving now circling for cover; his shield was weakened by the blasts of the initial attack.

Seeing his attacker for the first time, Nico snarled through bloodied lips, "I told you never to touch me again!"

The force of his full weight crashed into Orion's midsection, carrying him off his feet. Nico's enhanced strength lifted him into the air and tossed him like a rag doll against the engine housing of the big truck. He smashed against the radiator, and hot steam scalded his back as he dropped to the ground and rolled. His gun was lost now and he knew that to go hand-to-hand against Nico's strength was chancy at best. Still, he drew both the assu khtra and leapt to his feet, poised to take another charge.

Nico did not disappoint, rushing him again like a maddened bull. This time Orion was ready and the blades bit deep into Nico's back as Orion's feet braced him against another throw. Again, like a bull, Nico bellowed with rage as blood shot up and out of the wounds.

Ripping one knife out of the injured brother's back, Orion spun the blade and plunged it into the top of Nico's skull. The viselike grip on Orion's waist loosened, and Nico slid to the floor.

Occupied as he was, Orion did not see Brock, now firing from cover and keeping the other men pinned down. Marco had watched their feet under the truck, looking for a way to help his brother. At the end, he had seen Nico fall to the floor, eyes empty and the assu khtra standing from his skull.

Screaming his brother's name, Marco fired wild beneath the truck, but Orion was too fast. With one leap he was on top the cab and then a second carried him into the men below, his size and weight scattering them like ten-pins.

Weaponless now, except for those that were a part of him, Orion ripped into the face of his nearest enemy with his claws and removed most of the man's ear and cheek.

Screaming and gushing blood, Orion was able to use the dead man as a shield when Marco started blasting in his direction. Seeing the blasts rip through his own man just drove Marco to new heights of frenzy, and he didn't see Brock walk up behind him until the lightning gun was against the back of his head. Brock fired, and the electrical arc took away half the surviving brothers face.

The remaining men lost all will to fight at that moment, dropping their weapons and raising their hands above them. Orion stood over Marco's body, claws dripping red gore and heard Brock mutter under his breath, "That's for O'Donal."

They collected the survivors and Brock covered them while Orion recovered his weapons. Brock called for backup while Orion checked the crates in the truck. "Wouldn't it be funny," the agent said, "If it turned out not to be weapons at all."

Orion pulled the slats off the top of the first crate and said, "No. Not funny."

All told, they found the largest cache of weapons recovered since the end of the conflict between the tir'a and the terrachians; masers, pulse rifles, even grenades and heavy lightning guns. Almost all were military grade and never meant for civilian hands.

As Brock's men and the locals mopped up and secured the weapons, while Orion and the agent shared a quiet moment.

"You're good to go, Marshal," Brock said. "Your reinstatement papers will be in the system by the time you get back to Midway."

"What about this?" Orion asked.

Brock looked around and said, "This? Oh, this never happened. You never were on Mars. There doesn't exist a single piece of evidence to the contrary. At least there won't be."

"Still didn't catch your mole."

"I will," he said, flashing that Cheshire cat grin again. "This was just part one. We took all this out of the hands of those two and Omak Shakti. This will hurt their bottom line. It's how you eat the elephant."

"Hmmm?"

"One bite at a time."

-- *The End*

About the Author

Clifford VanMeter began his career after college as an illustrator working in the role-playing game field. Early work included the Star Trek and Dr. Who role playing games, Battle-Tech, the DC Universe Role Playing Game, Chill, Traveller and much more.

Later he founded *Starchilde Studios* where he created, wrote and published the game Justifiers RPG.

Moving to New York to pursue work in comics, Cliff wrote and drew for Valiant Comics at the height of their popularity. Additional work came from Marvel, Milestone/DC Comics, and Image. He also started *Comicolor*, one of the first digital coloring and lettering companies for comic books in North America.

He lives and works in Kalamazoo, Michigan with his wife, and daughter. The Spiral Arm Stories Book One is his second published book.

Gallery

Some previously published and unpublished art by Cliff. See more at CliffordVanMeter.com.

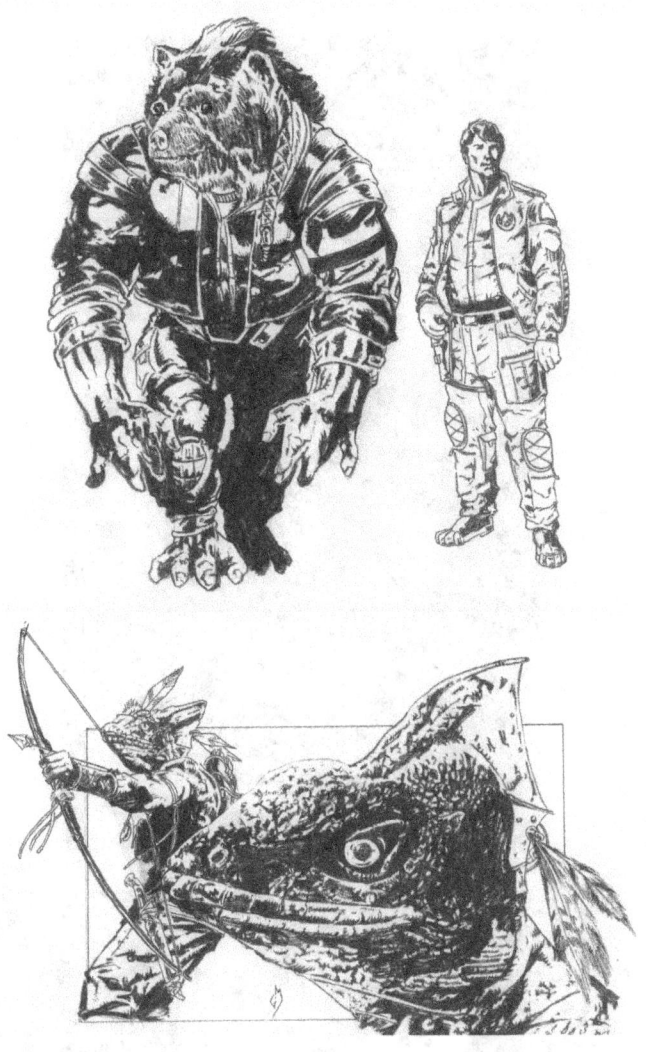

Top: komouch with constable.
Bottom: chrysanth.